JED HERNE

The Thunder Heist
(Twisted Seas #1)

Undergrove Press

Cover art by Ramón Ignacio Bunge
Twisted Seas logo by Tina Han
Editing by Rebekah Craggs
All other interior images by Jed Herne

Second edition

To Ma, with love.

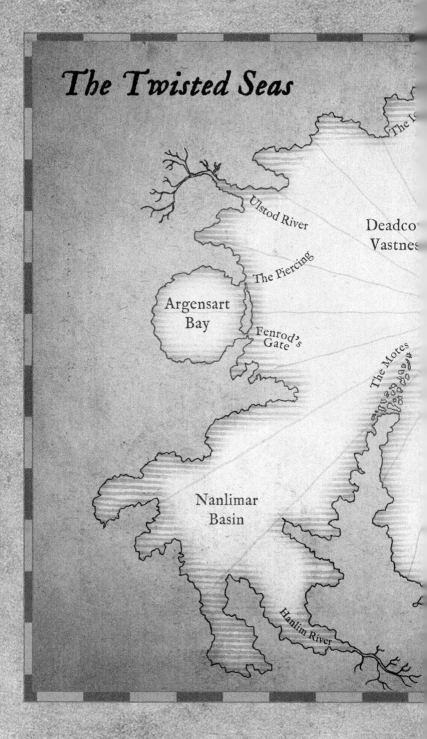

The Twisted Seas

The Ⅰ...

Ulstod River

Deadco...
Vastnes...

The Piercing

Argensart
Bay

Fenrod's
Gate

The Motes

Nanlimar
Basin

Hanlim River

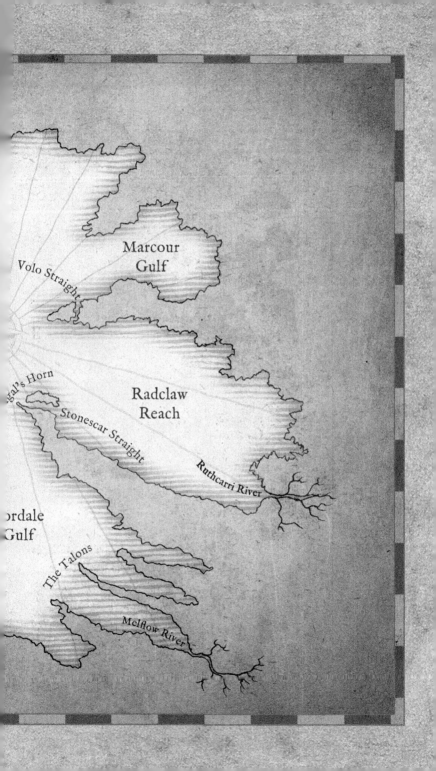

Visit <u>www.JedHerne.com/ThunderHeistArt</u> for
high-resolution copies of all art in this book.

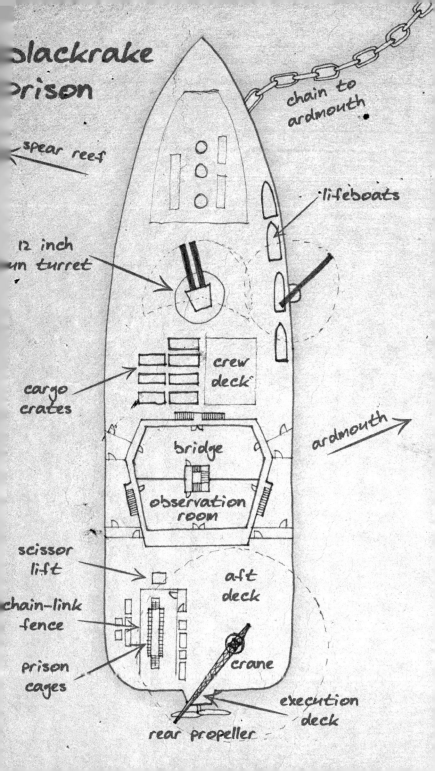

Blackrake
Prison

chain to ardmouth

spear reef

lifeboats

12 inch gun turret

crew deck

cargo crates

bridge

ardmouth

observation room

scissor lift

aft deck

chain-link fence

prison cages

crane

execution deck

rear propeller

Chapter 1: Blackrake Prison

Kef Cutmark opened her eyes. "Well. That's a damn disappointment."

In the cage next to hers, metal creaked as Gerald rolled over. "Talking about yourself?"

"Talking about today. Thought it'd feel special. Not every day you get executed."

Kef pushed herself up into a squat, yawning, then raked her fingers through her tangled, salt-matted hair to scratch the back of her neck. Damn vermin were crawling all over Blackrake Prison. And the bugs were pretty bad, too.

She stretched – if you could call it a stretch, when you were all folded up in a cage without room to stand. Her joints popped. She rolled her neck, easing out the kinks, while the floor swayed beneath her from the waves crashing against the ship's hull.

Last night, they'd pulled her out of the windowless cell belowdecks in the ship's belly. That was a pity, because she'd finally scrounged enough contraband playing cards to set up an illegal gambling den, right in the shadowy back corner that was either the perfect place to get shanked, or the best spot to sleep.

After pulling her from the cell, they'd shoved her into a cage more fit for a dog than a woman. She'd gone quietly, not like the other prisoners. They'd all done their pathetic best to prolong the moment, which was a stupid move, because it just meant they'd spend their last hours with bruises and broken bones. Still, Kef wasn't like the others. On a ship where everyone was desperate to delay their death, everyone was still wondering why she'd persuaded the guards to move her execution forward.

With Kef pressed up against the bars, they'd wheeled her cage along rusted metal walkways. Whenever the wheels hit a bump, the cage rattled hard enough to make Kef worry about losing a tooth. They slid her onto a platform, and then a wheezing scissor-lift elevated her onto the ship's main deck, where a crane lifted the cage to slot Kef's prison into a metal scaffold.

That was where she was now. Locked in a cage, dozens of condemned prisoners stacked around her – most in various degrees of concussion from their failed struggles last night.

The sun's pale light inched over the distant horizon, flickering as waves chopped across the sea. Several miles west of Blackrake Prison, the sharp rocky blades of the Spear Reef glistened red in the early morning glow, like tusks bathed in blood. As she squinted at the Reef, a gust of wind dampened her cheeks with sea-spray. She tasted salt on her tongue.

To the east, joined to Blackrake Prison by a long anchor, Ardmouth was waking to a new day. Like the other city-ships that sailed around the Twisted Seas, Ardmouth was made from lashed-together boats, ranging from huge tankers to tiny shanty vessels which were more rust than metal. Living on a floating city could be hard. But with the land around the Twisted Seas dominated by monsters who'd kill you before you could take three steps out of the water, even the scrappiest dingy in the dirtiest city-ship was preferable.

Saying that, plenty of monsters infested the seas, too. They were just slightly easier to deal with, although that depended on where you were. Most city-ships – including Ardmouth – drifted around the Fordale Gulf, where monsters were smaller and less aggressive. But if you sailed through a place like the Deadcour Vastness, you'd be lucky to reach the other side without a leviathan swallowing your vessel.

Hundreds of miles of chains criss-crossed Ardmouth, linking the boats and spreading out far under the water – a defence against pirates and sea monsters. On the decks of the tallest ship, a crowd of well-dressed civilians had gathered, all babbling excitedly and looking through binoculars at Blackrake Prison.

Kef snorted. One woman's death was another's breakfast entertainment. Soon, they'd probably let the rich bastards execute the prisoners themselves.

"Nice sunrise, at least," Kef said.

"Do you ever shut up?" Gerald asked from the cage beside her. "We're about to die and you're going on about the bloody view."

Kef turned to raise an eyebrow at her neighbour. He was hunched in a miserable ball, looking small and damp. When they'd tossed her into jail last week, she'd barely had time to fix her hair before Gerald tried to grope her.

She smirked. "How are the fingers?"

Gerald scowled down at his hands. His makeshift splints couldn't disguise how his thumb now looked like it had four knuckles. Annoyingly enough, when she'd broken them, he'd only grown more infatuated with her, but in an irritating,

3

puppy-dog way. She supposed he'd been useful to remove corpses from the best mattresses, but mostly he'd made her wish she'd snuck earplugs into the prison ship. Thankfully, getting pulled up to the decks for his execution seemed to have tempered his more annoying habits. Funny how death's presence had that effect.

"And by the way." Kef leaned back against the bars, watching the pale sun crawl out of the water. "Not to get too philosophical about it, 'cause I know that might explode your tiny brain, but this seems like the perfect time to appreciate it. It's the last sunrise you'll ever see."

"And yours, too."

Kef smiled. "Sure."

A bell toiled in the city, low and ominous. With groans and curses, the other caged prisoners woke. Some of them stuffed fingers into ears, but it did nothing to stop the bell's headache-inducing clang. Down on the decks below, the bleary-eyed night shift guards swapped places with the morning watch. The bell kept clanging.

"Cheer up, all." Kef grinned at the other prisoners. "By the next bell we'll all be dead!"

That sobered them for a second. Then there were the usual responses: curses, cries, people threatening to rip off her arms and shove them up her arse. She revelled in the noise, chuckling. Playing a crowd was all about taking advantage of their emotions. And there were no emotions quite as strong as fear.

Boots clanked on the walkway. Guards ran batons along the cage bars, shouting at prisoners to shut up. A sulky silence came over the inmates. Kef smirked. Why were they still afraid of authority? Did they think obedience would change

4

the guards' minds? When it came to following orders, people were fools.

Chief Warden Henderson emerged onto the walkway outside Kef's cage, scowling. He was a thickset, burly man, who was just as tough as the regular prison guards, and just as happy to beat unruly prisoners. Behind him flanked his two Lieutenants: Eames and Redfern.

Eames was a giller – a water-breathing mutant with slitted yellow eyes, webbed hands, and long bare feet, flat and stretched like flippers. With strong arms and broad shoulders, she towered over the guards around her. Beneath her grey overcoat, she wore a skin-tight swimsuit, designed to reduce drag in the water. The overcoat's collar was turned down to expose the gills on either side of her neck. They fluttered as she breathed.

Next to her, Redfern was short and slim. He was a winger: a mutant with clawed feet and wings sticking out from his shoulder-blades. Unlike Eames, who was all drab greys, Redfern wore a ruffled white shirt with a high collar, and dozens of red silk tassels hung from his leather belt. When he flew, they would stream out behind him, rippling like a flag in the wind.

Rumour was that they'd both been prisoners, but had repented after stopping an escape attempt from another inmate, earning Henderson's respect. Kef smirked. Repentance. More likely they'd just enjoyed hurting people, and working for the Warden gave plenty of chances for that.

Warden Henderson surveyed the prisoners. "Cuff them."

Guards strode along the walkways, opening slots in the cages to lock handcuffs around prisoners' wrists. When people tried to resist, guards shoved open the door, then barged inside to bludgeon them with batons.

A guard with a crooked grin slid open the slot in Kef's cell. "Hands here, pretty."

The guard's own hand rested on the slot, handcuffs held with lazy fingers. Kef thought about all the ways she could wrench those fingers against the bar, levering them until they snapped. Instead, she smiled up at the guard, allowing him to slap cold manacles around her wrists. His skin brushed hers.

"Ouch!"

The guard flinched back, frowning down at his hand.

Another guard rushed over. "You alright, Ben?"

"Fine. Just an electric shock."

The guards unlocked her cage, then dragged her out. Standing upright made blood drain from her head. Spots danced before her eyes. Kef swayed as they marched her along the walkway, then down the stairs. As they rounded a landing, she slipped over, her arms knocking into the legs of the guard and the prisoner in front of her. They stumbled, cursing. Firm hands grabbed her arms, hauling her up. She was more careful this time, and they didn't even notice the static electricity pass between them as their skin touched.

They stepped down onto the deck. Her balance was back now, and she managed the sway of the ground beneath her with no troubles as the guards formed the prisoners up into a line. Today, eight were scheduled for execution. Gerald was a few spots behind her, his posture slumped enough that despite his height, he was shorter than the old woman behind him, who wore circular optics. She'd been one of the few prisoners who hadn't struggled. Not that it would've done much good, since she looked to be in her late seventies. Maybe living a long life made you less worried about it ending.

Guards marched them through the maze of scaffolding that held the prisoners' cages. Jeers and spittle rained down from above. Kef glared up at the prisoners still stacked high in their cages.

"You'll get your turn, you bastards," she shouted.

The boos grew louder. Kef shook her head. Didn't they see how stupid it all was? An extra day in the cage wouldn't improve their lives, but sometimes that was all survival was: outlasting the day, the hour, the minute.

The cages were stacked tall on the deck, surrounded by a rectangle of chain-link fence topped with barbed wire coils. Leading them through several gates, none of which were opened at the same time, the guards marched the prisoners out of the compound. When they reached the base of the crane that had lifted Kef's cage last night, the Warden barked an order. They stopped in a neat line.

Distorted cheers sounded from Ardmouth. Kef glanced towards her left. On the distant ship decks, sunlight glinted off binoculars. The mouth-watering smells of roasted nuts, baked pies, and other fair-ground foods wafted across the sea. Her stomach grumbled. She hadn't eaten a decent meal in a week.

She turned her focus back to the prison ship as doors slammed open. Up on the bridge, which loomed above the aft deck, well-tailored men and women emerged to look down at the prisoners. Honourborns. Some held flutes of champagne, while others munched on canapes. How much had they paid for a courtside view? Their position had the added benefit of being highly visible to all the observers from the distant city. What better way to show that you cared about order, and were damn well-dressed, too?

7

Guards stood beside the honourborns, with rifles held by their sides. Legal attendants balanced notepads on the railing, ready to record the deaths – or as they called it, justice. In Kef's experience, they weren't much different.

"We are gathered here on this Fallsday morning," said the Warden in a booming voice, "To sentence those who would breach the laws of the sea."

Kef ignored his words as he continued. Nothing she hadn't heard before. Taking a deep breath, she directed her focus inwards. While walking, she'd brushed against a dozen or so people, but it hadn't been enough. She needed more.

As the Warden strode past her, prattling about order and justice and a load of other tripe, she reached out and touched his lips. Her dirty finger smeared grime over his skin.

"Shush," she said.

For a second, everyone gaped at her. Then five guards tackled Kef, slamming her against the metal structure that supported the crane. She tried to raise her arms to defend herself, but they pinned her down and smashed kicks into her torso. Pain flared through her. She hissed, hands clenching into fists, forcing herself not to fight back.

The guards cleared aside, making way for the Warden to tower over her, his left eye twitching. He grabbed a baton from a guard, then smashed it into Kef's skull, sending light exploding behind her eyes.

"For that, you can go first."

Kef grinned up at him, blood dribbling down from her split lip. "My pleasure."

The prisoners looked at her with pitiful eyes. Gerald chuckled, and when she flipped him off, he only laughed harder. Next to him the old woman shook her head.

8

The guards dragged Kef's limp body upright. She stumbled, but managed to grab the crane's frame for support. Her right hand fell on the power cable. She closed her eyes, concentrating, but didn't get more than a second before the guards ripped her away. They marched her to the ship's aft. She groaned. Everything ached. Maybe it had been stupid to go for the Warden when simply brushing another guard would do. But it wouldn't have been as fun.

They took her onto a deck that stuck out from the ship's aft. Far below, waves slapped against the hull. Water churned in a savage eddy and the propeller's blades flicked spray into the air. Most ships kept their propeller well below the water, for safety. A long time ago, Blackrake Prison had modified their rear propeller so that the top half stuck out of the water. Not the most efficient way to execute prisoners, but it sure was dramatic. Kef had to give them points for that. There wasn't even the option of diving into the water – gillers swam around the ship, armed with spearguns and ready to finish any prisoners who weren't mangled by the propeller.

"Kef Cutmark," said a woman's voice.

Kef glanced up, flicking her head to get the hair out of her eyes. An imperious woman dressed in a dark gown stood on the bridge, her face hidden behind a black mask that covered everything except her eyes and mouth. A dark purple sash stretched across her chest – the mark of an Ardmouth judge.

"Let this court witness the sentencing of Kef Cutmark." The Judge looked at her notes. "Also known as Janice Claw-Arm, also known as Mary the Red, also known as the Raider of the Far Reach, also known as …"

It went on for some time. Kef yawned. The Judge reached the end of the page, turned over, saw more names, and sighed.

"… and other aliases, henceforth." The Judge took a deep breath. "Kef Cutmark stands accused of thirty-two cases of assault, twenty-five cases of extortion, seventeen cases of piracy and theft, six cases of property damage …"

The other prisoners gaped at Kef as the Judge continued to read. Kef took that as a compliment. She'd lived more life than most people ever did, and she was only twenty-nine. Mind you, that was above average for a woman in her line of work.

The Judge flipped the page. This time, a determined note entered her voice, and she kept reading until all of the crimes had been spoken.

Kef nodded. "Not bad. You almost got half of them."

She couldn't see the Judge's face behind her mask, but she sensed that the woman was glaring.

"Your guilt has been decided," said the Judge. "This is merely a sentencing hearing. However, as by the rites of law, you may make one final statement. Do you have anything to say for yourself?"

Kef shrugged. "You forgot to mention my looks."

She shone a dazzling smile at a few gentlemen in the crowd, which made them blush and glance away guiltily, much to the annoyance of their female companions.

"Oh," Kef said. "And fuck you, Judge."

The prisoners laughed. Back in the cages, the other inmates rattled the bars, joining in.

"For these crimes," shouted the Judge while guards quietened the prisoners, "Kef Cutmark is sentenced to execution. Guards, activate the crane."

The honourborns cheered. A guard climbed up the crane's ladder, crawling into the operator's cabin. Excitement rippled through the crowd. The crane's hook would lock around Kef's handcuffs, and then it would lower her over the side and onto the propeller. The hook was unpickable. And even if she slipped out of her handcuffs and dove into the water, a giller's speargun would make short work of her. Still, that would beat the propeller. They'd lower her slowly, and rumours claimed that Warden Henderson had calculated the perfect way to keep prisoners alive until the blades sawed through to the chest.

On the deck of the prison ship, everything was quiet, save for the lapping of waves against the hull. High above in the operator's cabin, there was a loud click as a key entered the ignition. Machinery hummed as the crane came to life. Its arm angled down, falling fast.

Too fast.

The arm swivelled to the side with a jerking motion. It bounced backwards, jerking up again, and then it changed direction once more, spasming like a caught fish. On the bridge, the honourborns stumbled back, shrieking.

"Control yourself!" barked the Warden at the operator.

"It's fighting me!" the operator yelled.

There was a clang as he ripped something open.

The operator cursed. "The circuits – they're fried!"

Down on the deck, Kef smiled.

The crane swung clockwise and the arm jerked down. It smashed through the chain-link fence, then crashed into the stacks of cages. With a cacophony of falling metal, the scaffolding broke apart.

Cages rained from the sky, smashing into the fence, slamming onto the deck, crushing shrieking prisoners in the lower levels. The ones who'd been higher were luckier. Their cages crashed into the ground, splitting open. Prisoners tumbled onto the deck.

Before the guards could close their gaping mouths, the freed prisoners sprinted towards them, wrestling the guards to the deck and stealing their weapons. Redfern and Eames shepherded Henderson away from the fight – Redfern lashed out with his wings to knock away a prisoner who got too close. They darted into a corridor, then slammed the door shut. Two prisoners hurled a guard into the door with a thunderous crash that dented the metal. Kef laughed. There was nothing quite like being caged to enrage an animal. Which reminded her – it was time to move.

She spun, twisting to kick the guard next to her. He staggered back. Pushing off the kick's momentum, she whipped her manacled hands over the other guard's neck, pulling the handcuffs up against his throat. He tried to struggle but she kneed him in the kidneys.

"Move and I'll break your neck," Kef snarled.

The other guard lurched back, lunging towards Kef. She twisted under his weight, using his momentum to send him crashing into the handrail. With a shove, Kef toppled him over the side. He screamed as he fell towards the spinning propeller. There was a nasty whine and a splattering of chopped meat as the blades did their grisly work. Trapped in Kef's grip, the remaining guard cursed in a muffled voice. He dribbled onto Kef's hands.

An alarm split the air with a high-pitch whine. Back on the main deck, a full-scale riot had broken out – prisoners and guards, grappling and stabbing, using knives and swords and batons.

Up on the bridge, a dozen guards had their rifles aimed at the chaos, but the melee was too jumbled for them to get clean shots. Then they saw Kef, standing with her handcuff's chain across a guard's neck, separated from the rioting crowd. Their rifles turned towards her.

Her captive guard cursed. "Don't shoot! You'll hit me!"

The rifles lowered. The guard breathed out in relief.

"That bitch messed with the crane!" yelled one of the riflemen. "She touched the power cable – I think she cut it!"

Their rifles tilted back up.

"So much for loyalty," said Kef.

Kef swung the guard in front of her as the rifles boomed. Bullets tore into the screaming man. She kept him held ahead as she charged towards the crane, blocking the bullets, wincing when the killing shot reduced the man to two hundred pounds of dead weight. When she reached the cover of the crane's base, she dumped the guard, then rummaged through his belt. Baton, knife – no gun. Damn. Made sense, though. You wouldn't want to risk prisoners stealing a ranged weapon. Only the snipers on the bridge would have those.

Kef glanced over at the brawling prisoners and guards. The prisoners had the upper hand, even though a decent number were hiding instead of fighting, or using stolen keys to race into the ship's hold. She saw Gerald hiding between two cargo crates, with the old woman crouching behind him. Good. Kef's target was safe. Although to reach them, she'd have to cross in full view of the snipers. Not a good move.

Instead, she climbed the crane's support frame, trusting that the dense structure would protect her from the snipers. Her boots slid on the slippery metal, almost sending her flying off the frame, but she gritted her teeth and clamped her hands around the steel with all her strength. This was her only way up. Getting inside to the access ladder was impossible, because the bars were spaced too closely together for security. That served her well, though, because the tightly spaced bars blocked Kef from the snipers.

High above, the crane's arm kept spasming. It swayed near the bridge several times, but it was too short to smash into the balcony.

Kef reached the top of the frame, then jumped onto the spinning operator cabin, grabbing the exterior handle. Inside, the guard's eyes bulged. Kef drew back her arm and with a furious swing, she smashed her baton against the windshield. The impact jolted up her arm. Spiderweb cracks raced out from her blow. She hit the windshield again, and again, and on the fourth try the glass shattered.

Kef crawled inside, slapping away the guard's feeble defences. She ripped off his keys before hurling him screaming out through the window. Then she ducked down behind the cover of the dashboard as bullets sprayed through the cabin, sending fragments of glass raining down around her.

She used her stolen knife to pry the maintenance panel open. Judging by the scratches on the metal, the operator had tried to do the same, but he'd lacked her strength. The acrid stench of melted wires greeted her. Screwing up her forehead, she searched for the manual circuit breaker, trying to remember the electrical diagrams she'd studied. There – by the sagging green wires. She glanced over the dash, waited until the crane arm was angled so that the end was fifteen feet above the bridge's balcony, and only three feet away from it. Then she yanked on the circuit breaker.

With a shriek of metal, the crane froze. The long metal cord swayed in the breeze, slapping against the bridge's railing as the hooked end came to a scraping rest on the deck below

– forming a perfect climbing rope from deck to bridge. A prisoner dashed for the rope, only for a barrage of gunfire to slice her down. But then there was another, and then three more, and then they were scrambling up the rope as the snipers struggled to reload.

Kef grinned as prisoners swarmed onto the bridge. Snipers dropped their rifles. They tried to flee inside, but the doors were locked. Prisoners grabbed the snipers' guns, whooping.

A powerful horn-blast shook the air. Kef whipped around. Three dreadnaughts were approaching Blackrake Prison, with eight wingers flying above it. Dozens of tiny speedboats raced around the fleet, each with gun turrets mounted to their prows.

"Prisoners of Blackrake!" boomed an amplified voice from the lead dreadnaught. "The military might of Ardmouth approaches. Surrender now or suffer our wrath!"

On the deck below, the prisoners kept pummelling the guards. Outside the bridge, the others slammed their rifles against the doors and the now-shuttered windows, denting the metal. There would be no easy surrender today. All the prisoners knew that capture meant death, so they fought with the frenzy of the condemned.

Kef opened the cabin's trapdoor. She slithered down the ladder inside the crane's support structure, landing on the deck with a thud. Around her, the close-spaced bars of the frame felt like another prison. Except this time she was on the right side of the bars.

Using the operator's keys, she opened a gate built into the frame, letting her step out onto the deck. She dashed across to Gerald and the old woman. Gerald gaped at her. He opened his mouth, probably to say something stupid. Whatever it was, Kef never found out, because before he could speak she slammed the baton into his head. He collapsed, knocked out cold.

Behind him, the old woman adjusted her optics. "Great. Now who's going to block any bullets that come my way?"

The woman spoke in a clipped tone, with a calm firmness despite the chaos unfolding around her. Her grey hair was pulled into a tight bun. She looked about the right age to be someone's grandmother, but the steeliness in her eyes and her rigid jawline made Kef think she had more in common with a drill sergeant.

"Gabine Ruth?" Kef asked, extending a hand to help her up.

The old woman stood by herself, frowning. "What do you want?"

"The same thing you do, I presume. I'm here to free you."

Chapter 2: Waves and Wrath

"I know you're probably curious," said Kef as she slammed a guard against the corridor's wall. "But I'm –"

The guard twisted, locking his hands around her neck.

"– kind of –"

Kef wriggled out of his grip, diving to grab the knife she'd dropped.

"– busy –"

The guard yanked her hair, pulling her up, and she used the momentum to drive the knife up through his chin and into his brain.

"– at the moment."

Kef pushed the guard aside. His limp body slumped onto the floor, next to the other guard she'd killed. She rummaged through his clothes, pulling out his purse and his knives. Further back along the corridor, Gabine Ruth raised her eyebrows.

"Quite understandable," said the old woman in a dry voice.

"I'll explain when we're out of this," said Kef. "Come on."

Gabine followed Kef, her arms folded behind her back. Kef had to respect the old woman; Gabine didn't even flinch as she stepped over the guard's bodies.

Kef strode through the corridor, knife in one hand, baton

in the other. She hadn't yet found a gun, which was annoying. Still, she didn't need one to escape. The other inmates had broken belowdecks to free the remaining prisoners, which meant this corridor should be almost empty.

They reached a door bearing a sign that said: *Quick-Access Bay 004.* Kef rattled the handle. The door was locked.

"What happened to your hand?" Gabine asked.

Kef glanced down. The rest of her was well-tanned, but there was a large pale patch on the back of her left hand. Only a smattering of freckled dots took it halfway towards matching her normal skin tone.

"Alchemical accident," she said, which was partly true.

Kef slid her stolen knife into the door's seam, feeling the tip hit the striking plate. Then she levered the knife to slide the spring-loaded latch back towards the handle. With a click, the lock opened. Kef straightened up. That wouldn't have worked with a proper lock, but this was an internal door with weak security – just like her informant had promised. Kicking open the door, she emerged into a small room.

Three jetboats sat on rails in dry dock bays. Unlike normal propeller-powered boats, jetboats drew water from under the hull through an intake. Then, an internal pump-jet shot the pressurised water through a nozzle at the back. Combined with the flat planing hull, low windshield, and sleek lines, these vessels were designed for speed.

Beneath the jetboats, rails angled down towards the far wall. Judging by the curve and from the metal ribs latticed across the wall, it was an openable section of the outer hull.

Supply lockers stood beside the entry door. Chairs clustered in the corner, with a handful of battered playing cards littered on the floor, but there were no guards. They'd all been called off to fight the riot, just like she'd anticipated. Excellent.

Kef pointed to the nearest boat. "Get in, Gabine."

Kef opened a locker. It held orange life vests, oil-stained coats, a coil of frayed rope, and a splotchy drawing of a girl, taped to the door. Kef ripped the drawing apart. Behind it, bare metal stared back at her.

"Shit," she said.

"What is it?" asked Gabine.

Kef glanced at her. Gabine swung her leg up over the side of the boat, then gasped and clutched her thigh. She stumbled away from the boat. Annoyance surged through Kef, but then she remembered this woman was in her seventies. Her wits were sharp, but she couldn't move as fast as Kef. That better not become a liability.

Kef tossed the rope, coats, and life vests into the boat, then slammed the locker shut with a bang. "I paid a guy to leave keys here. They're not."

Kef pulled a lever next to the lockers. With a groan of pistons, the curving side wall slid up, opening to reveal water lapping against the hull seven feet below. Kef raced to the speedboat, vaulting over the side.

Her foot slid on a hooked pole that skittered out from underneath her, but she landed on the deck without falling. Luckily, she'd missed the hook. That metal looked sharp.

Gabine kept struggling to get in, so Kef dragged her up and over the side. The old woman stumbled onto the first mate's seat, wincing and massaging her leg. Good thing she didn't cry. Kef had no time for criers.

The exit door came to a halt with a thunderous crash. On the speedboat, Kef pried the casing off the steering console. She fiddled with the wires underneath.

19

"There's boats outside," Gabine said. "Heading towards us."

Kef looked over the console. She had to squint because of the low-angled early morning light, which reflected off the sharp tips of the Spear Reef on the horizon. Three interceptors skimmed across the water in the distance, curving around to point at Kef and Gabine. These were jetboats, too, with vicious rams mounted on their prows.

Kef's heartbeat quickened as she ducked back under the console to tinker with the wires.

"Gabine, tie something around your head to mask your face. They can't know you've escaped."

Fabric tore as the old woman set to work.

"They're coming towards us," Gabine said in a gruff voice. "We've got thirty, maybe thirty-five seconds."

She sounded calm despite the approaching threat. Good judge of distances, too. Just what you would've expected, given the woman's former job.

Sparks flared between the wires. Kef ducked out of the dashboard as the engine roared to life. She raced to the back of the boat, pleased to see that Gabine had covered her face with a wrapping that showed only her eyes.

Kef untied the mooring rope, then heaved against the dry dock's frame. With a low groan, the jetboat slid down the steel tracks, picking up speed as it raced towards the opening.

"Hold on!" Kef said as she slid into the captain's chair, glancing to check that Gabine was sitting firm in the other seat.

The boat shot out of the dry dock, falling through the air. Weightlessness filled Kef. The hull slammed into the sea, water crashing over the sides to swamp the deck and chill Kef's ankles. For a second she worried they'd sink. Then the pump-jet roared to life, petrol-smoke filled Kef's nostrils, and the boat shot away from Blackrake Prison, sending water sloshing off the back.

Kef turned the wheel. The hooked pole slid across the floor with a clatter as the boat curved around to the left. A half-mile away, the navy interceptors angled to cut her off. She narrowed her eyes. No boat-mounted weapons, although the crew probably had guns. Against big ships, those interceptors were practically useless. When hunting little boats like Kef's, however, they were deadly. Even with a dozen crew on each interceptor, they were as fast as Kef's vessel, and that ram could split her boat in two.

The interceptors roared towards Kef. Soldiers stood on their decks, raising rifles to firing positions. Within seconds they'd be close enough to shoot, and with Kef's portside exposed, she'd be an easy target for ramming.

"Get your head down," she said to Gabine. "And if you've got any gods, pray to them."

Grunting, Gabine ducked, hooking one arm around her seat and using her other hand to keep her optics from falling off. Kef yanked the wheel. The speedboat tilted to the side, spraying water into the air and turning until it pointed headfirst at the approaching interceptors.

She slammed the throttle forward.

Petrol-smoke crawled up her nostrils and with a howl of power the boat blasted towards the closest interceptor. The soldiers' rifles trembled. She grinned, leaning low over the wheel, relishing the salty mist spraying across her face.

Feeble gunshots sent bullets arcing over Kef's head. Before they could get a proper bead on her, their captains turned the interceptors away, trying to avoid her path. As they turned, they exposed their starboard sides. Kef angled towards the nearest interceptor. A collision at this speed would destroy a boat – but which one?

Soldiers cursed. They dropped their rifles and braced for impact. Kef took her jetboat close enough to read the names on their uniforms, and then she angled to the side, sending her gliding past one boat's prow and spraying water over the crew.

As Kef's jetboat skimmed away across the water, she turned to grin at the stunned soldiers. "Nice try, you bastards!"

Their boats wheeled around to follow, but she'd put a nice head start between them.

"Can I get up?" asked Gabine, who was sprawled on the ground. "If you're done showing off."

"Hey, don't sound too grateful. Not like I just saved your life."

Scowling, Gabine clambered up to sit in the first mate's chair. "You haven't saved it yet. There's three boats behind us and nothing but open sea ahead."

"Not quite, there's –" Kef frowned at the woman. "What's going on there?"

The woman looked down at her hand, which was pressed against her heaving chest, right over her heart.

"What?" Gabine asked.

Gabine's voice was firm. Angry, even, like Kef was stupid for asking. If Kef didn't know better, she would have sworn the old woman was fine. But Kef had far too much experience with pretending things were fine to let Gabine dupe her.

"You're not having a heart attack, are you?"

"No!" The woman paused. "I don't think so, but my family has a history –"

"Well calm down! Do you know how long this took to set up?"

"I do not."

"Then fucking calm down!"

"I'd be calmer if you told me the plan."

Kef pointed to a patch on the horizon darkened by storm clouds, where sharp fangs of reef rose through the waves and sunlight reflected off moss-slicked rocks.

"We'll lose them there."

The old woman gaped. "That's the Spear Reef! You can't go there in a storm. That's suicide, you fool!"

"Gabine, you thought you were going to die an hour ago, and look how that turned out. Have a little faith."

Kef glanced over her shoulder. The interceptors had narrowed the gap, skimming along in her wake. They were maybe a third of a mile away. Some of the tension eased out of Kef's muscles. Her jetboat would reach the Spear Reef before the interceptors got within gun range, unless they pulled out some sort of surprise.

From the deck of Blackrake Prison, two figures leapt off the side. One man, one woman. The woman flashed down towards the water, diving into the waves without so much as a splash despite the seventy-foot drop.

Wings extended from behind the man's back. His dive levelled out and then he soared towards Kef and Gabine, wings moving so fast they almost blurred.

"Ah, dammit," said Kef. "Gabine, take the wheel."

"What?"

"Eames and Redfern. They're coming for us."

Kef let go. Gabine scrambled out of her seat, grabbing onto the wheel with white-knuckled hands. Redfern was still three

23

quarters of a mile away, but with the wind at his back, he was gaining ground. Down in the water, Kef couldn't see Eames, but she knew the giller would be shooting towards them just as fast.

"What do I do?" Gabine asked.

"Point us at the Reef. Shout when you're thirty seconds away."

Clouds blackened the sky as they neared the Reef. Kef rummaged through the boat. She'd paid the guard to hide a gun in the captain's drawers, but when she couldn't find it, she wasn't surprised. Damn bastard. Luckily, there was a weapon of a different sort. Kef grabbed it, then straightened up.

She tapped the bottle against Gabine's elbow. "Cheers!"

Kef drained the rum in one long draw. The woody taste felt glorious as it passed over her tongue. Probably one of the spiced varieties made from the floating plantations in the Nanlimar Basin. Or just an alchemical fake. Either way, she didn't care.

The old woman gaped. "You made me take the wheel so you could drink?"

Kef finished the bottle, then smacked her lips. "Don't stop now. You're doing great."

She held the empty bottle with her mouth, then shrugged a life vest over her shoulders. Next, she grabbed the rope coiled on the deck. After tying a loop around her ankle, she lashed the other end to a cleat. If she fell off the boat, that would make it easier to get back on board. Although if she dropped into the water, she wouldn't last long against the giller.

Transferring the bottle to her right hand, she grabbed the hooked pole from the ground. Sunlight glinted off the sharp metal. With a slight wobble to her steps, she strode to the boat's stern, the rope around her ankle dragging behind her.

Redfern flew over the pursuing jetboats. Attached to his belt, his silk tassels streamed out behind him. Now that he was closer, Kef saw a gun in his right hand and a hooked spear in his left – a more deadly version of Kef's own fishing hook. Eames was the real threat, though. Hidden under the water, the giller could attack from anywhere and Kef would have no warning.

"Alright." Kef tightened her grip on the empty rum bottle. "When they get close, the winger will try shooting us, or pulling us off the boat with his hooked spear. Keep us moving erratically. Zigzags, random direction changes – got it?"

Gabine sighed. "Too late to go back to prison?"

Kef laughed.

Redfern soared towards them. Kef waited until the winger pulled overhead, aiming his gun at her.

"Now!"

The deck tilted as the boat swayed to the side, angling away from the winger. His startled gunshots peppered the water.

"Keep waving!" said Kef. "Don't let him get a fix on us."

Redfern adjusted course, soaring back above the boat. He holstered his gun. Smart choice. Hitting a moving target while you were flying through the air wasn't easy. Using his spear would be simpler.

Redfern dove towards Kef. She hurled the empty rum bottle at him, which smashed into his chest, making him falter. It didn't have the same effectiveness as the throwing knives she liked to use, but surprise could make any tool deadly. Especially given the winger's hollow bones – good for flying, bad for taking hits.

Trying to recover from the blow, the winger's altitude dropped. Kef jumped, reaching up with her hooked pole. Redfern's wings beat at the last moment, sending him up into the air and out of her range. Her hook swished past his ankle.

Kef ducked, waiting for the return blow. Instead, Redfern soared over her, towards Gabine. Kef cursed. If anything happened to the old woman, this mission was bust.

The winger pivoted in the air, his clawed foot lashing towards Gabine's head. She yanked the steering wheel to the right. The boat spun around. Swung by the movement towards the winger, Kef crashed into his side, grappling with his writhing legs.

Redfern's foot-talons slashed through her life vest, spilling foam and slicing across her chest. She gritted her teeth against the pain. His wings cuffed her head and he tried to flap away from her, but she was too heavy for him. She wrestled Redfern down and slammed him against the deck. Bones crunched. Redfern screamed and his wings spasmed, curling around to hug Kef.

She grabbed a knife from her belt, struggling against his constricting wings. Redfern's hands scratched her face. She slapped them away, then jammed the knife into his temple and heard his skull crunch.

Blood spurted across her hand. Redfern's wings flopped to the deck, freeing Kef. Panting, she tossed him overboard. His corpse skipped along the water's surface and loose feathers fluttered into the air as Kef's boat drew away.

A body erupted from the water beside the jetboat. Eames crashed into Kef, sending her tumbling over the gunwale. Kef almost fell overboard, but somehow she hooked her toes under a cleat, leaving her dangling head-first over the starboard side.

Eames' webbed fingers wrapped around Kef's neck, forcing her head down towards the churning water. Kef struggled. Water sprayed into her eyes, making her squint. At this speed, hitting the roaring water would be like headbutting steel. The giller bared her teeth. From where Kef was, she had no leverage to push back and as soon as she went under, Eames would have all the power.

"Thirty seconds to the Reef!" shouted Gabine.

Kef cursed. Spit dribbled from her mouth, whipped away by the wind. She let go of Eames' choking hands, searching her body for a knife. Nothing. Must've fallen out when the giller tackled her. Eames forced Kef closer to the water. The woman grinned. Kef was going under and there was no way around it.

Kef's fingers brushed her ankle, touching the rope she'd tied there earlier. Inspiration struck her. She grabbed the rope with her left hand, seized the giller's hair with her right, and then unhooked her toes from beneath the cleat.

They toppled overboard. Kef twisted as she fell, tucking her chin to her chest. Water slapped into her back, hard as a hammer, and the giller fell onto her. They skimmed across the surface in a writhing tangle of limbs. The speedboat shot away and the giller leered, but then Kef looped her rope around the woman's neck. Eames' face paled.

The rope yanked on Kef's ankle, pulling them both along in the jetboat's wake. Water sprayed out from behind the vessel, splattering Kef as she tugged on the rope, choking Eames. The giller tried to slip her fingers underneath the rope, but it was too tight, cutting into her flesh and drawing blood from her gills. Eames' yellow eyes rolled into the back of her head.

"Twenty seconds!" shouted Gabine. "I have to slow down!"

27

Kef glanced behind her. The interceptors had closed the distance.

"No!" Kef said. "Stay at full speed!"

She gripped onto the rope, clambering over the dead giller to haul herself into a standing position. Water slammed into her bare feet, spraying up onto the inside of her thighs. Kef twisted her feet inward, sending the spray away from her, then slid her hand further along the rope, pulling herself towards the jetboat with straining muscles. Kef swore. There were fifteen feet of rope between her and the boat. She'd never make it in time.

Gunshots boomed behind her. Above, the darkening sky rumbled with thunder and wind howled through the air. Bad conditions for flying, which would hopefully stop any more wingers following them.

"Fifteen seconds! Kef, I can't –"

"Pull the lever next to the wheel! The yellow one!"

Gabine shifted into reverse. The boat slowed and the rope slackened, sending Kef skimming forward, carried by her momentum. She slammed into the aft, toppling over onto the deck.

Kef staggered forward, almost slipping on the water-soaked floor. "Move!"

Gabine stumbled aside. She strapped herself into the first mate's chair as Kef slid into the captain's seat. Waves leapt over the prow, soaking Kef with bone-chilling coldness as she slammed the yellow lever forward, regaining their lost speed. The sharp needles of the Spear Reef were only a few hundred feet away. Although from this distance, they looked less like needles and more like the fangs of a giant sea monster.

A wave tossed the jetboat into the air. Kef's feet lifted

off the ground. If it wasn't for her grip on the wheel, she would've been hurled overboard. Muscles straining, she wrenched herself back into the captain's seat right before the boat slammed into the water. The impact rattled her teeth.

They burst through a wave. A sharp outcrop of reef appeared, slick with algae and bigger than their entire boat. Gabine yelled. Kef twisted the steering wheel, sending the boat skimming past the rock, scraping along the surface with a horrible shriek.

Sharp spikes of reef pierced up from the water around them. When waves ripped apart the water, more spikes appeared, buried just under the surface. Kef wove between the deadly reef, frowning in concentration. Waves wrestled against her control, but she somehow kept them gliding through the Spear Reef without their boat breaking apart.

Soldiers screamed as an interceptor smashed into a rock. She glanced over her shoulder to see a boat splinter apart, tossing crew members into the air. The other interceptors pulled away from the reef. None of their captains were stupid enough to follow their fallen comrades.

Kef turned her focus back towards the prow. The Spear Reef extended for twenty miles. If the interceptors weren't going to follow her now, they wouldn't catch her when she came out the other side.

Gabine's face was pale. Kef didn't blame her. If anything, she had to give the woman credit for keeping herself inside the boat.

"Cheer up!" Kef slapped the old woman's shoulder. "We're free now. Wasn't that easy?"

Gabine's chest heaved. She gaped as Kef continued steering the boat between the reef, slower now that they weren't being chased.

"Easy?" Gabine spluttered. "You called that easy?"

"Of course." Kef pointed up at the fading storm. "Didn't even need that."

"What … what's next?"

"Next?" Kef smiled. "Well, it's time to find out if freeing you was worth it."

Chapter 3: Return to Zorith

Lightning forked through the air, slashing down from storm clouds to strike a spire in the middle of the city-ship. A few seconds later, thunder boomed.

Waves slapped against the jetboat as Kef stopped the vessel a mile away from Zorith. "We're here, Gabine."

Grumbling, the old woman's eyes blinked open and she sat up from the pile of life vests she'd used as a makeshift bed. When she saw the city, her eyes widened.

Kef smiled. "I thought you'd recognise it."

Gabine snorted. "You could say that."

Another bolt of lightning shot from the sky, striking the spire atop a soaring tower. Like Ardmouth, Zorith was made from a cluster of boats, welded and lashed and chained together to form a sprawling metropolis that bobbed on the waves with echoing groans of creaking metal. The great pleasure ship at the city's bow was big enough to hold Blackrake Prison three times over inside its belly, while towards the stern were vessels no larger than Kef's jetboat, sandwiched between blocky cargo tankers, like suckerfish attached to sharks.

Amongst the dark night-time water, the city glowed. Even from this distance, Kef heard the striking of metal, the pounding of footsteps clanking across walkways, and the hum of voices. Clouds of smoke billowed up from factory chimneys, catching the light. While most city-ships relied on prana oil for power – which meant they were constantly roving across the Twisted Seas in search of new seabeds to mine – long ago Zorith had developed a way to harness a different power. The power of the storms themselves.

Another lightning bolt struck the tallest spire. White light flashed across Gabine's face, illuminating her wrinkles and revealing the recognition in her eyes. Kef hadn't yet told her the full plan, but the old woman was putting the pieces together, as expected.

"I don't know what you want," said Gabine. "But I –"

"We'll talk later. When we're alone."

Gabine frowned. "Alone?"

A woman burst from the water, landing on the deck. Gabine flinched. Kef nodded to the giller, who wore a dark swimsuit. Zorith's symbol was emblazoned on the suit in blue-and-white: a spear rising from a wave, with a flag rippling under the point, and a slightly tilted set of balance scales sticking out from the shaft, just under the flag. If the scales tipped any further in either direction, they'd dip into the water. Two knives lined the giller's belt – one heavy and serrated, one thin like a skewer. A speargun was slung over her shoulder and the sharp metal tip gleamed from the city's lights.

"State your business, Captain," said the giller in a silky voice, water dripping from her shiny body onto the deck.

"Request to dock at Metteract Harbour," said Kef. "I have some trading to do in Zorith."

She and Gabine weren't dressed as nicely as most captains were, but at least they'd thrown their prison rags overboard a while ago, replacing them with jackets Kef had nicked from the storage locker in Blackrake. Wasn't great, but they'd pass. Acting was less about outfits and more about attitude.

"Your request is denied," said the giller. "Zorith is closed to visitors, on order of High Captain Exoran."

Kef frowned. "Who? I thought Callaghan was your High Captain."

"No longer. She was weak and did not heed the will of the people. High Captain Exoran will lead us to a new age of prosperity."

Kef chewed her lip. Only a week ago, Callaghan had been in charge, and now she was gone. Kef knew there'd been unrest, but still … what else had happened while she'd been in Blackrake?

"Look," she said. "I appreciate that a change of leadership can be hard, but we really do have urgent business in Zorith, and I don't want to disappoint my partners. You're welcome to search my boat. We have no weapons and we aren't here to be a nuisance."

The giller surveyed the boat through her slitted eyes. A distant lightning strike illuminated her face, revealing tiny scales across her cheeks. As her head turned, Kef glimpsed a tattoo on her throat – a symmetrical crossing of jagged lines. It was the mark of the Asadi, the order that bred, raised, and trained mutants, before loaning them out to the highest bidder. Asadi mutants didn't have a bad life, all things considered. But their life wasn't theirs, either. They were little more than indentured servants with few possessions or rights of their own.

Kef scratched her forehead. "Listen, I know you must be busy. I'm more than happy to supply a … processing fee, if that can speed up this affair."

The giller's eyes narrowed. "Of what price do you speak?"

Kef relaxed. Manipulating people was simply about the levers. All you had to do was find the right one, then pull.

She took a purse from her pocket. Kef had stolen it from one of the guards she'd killed in Blackrake Prison.

She opened the purse, then counted. "Fifty-five luras. Took me a good few days to earn these."

The giller licked her lips. "Ninety."

Kef opened the purse, showing its contents to the woman. "The most I've got is seventy."

"Then I'll take sixty-five."

"That's robbery!" said Gabine.

"I'm sure your associates in Zorith will be more than happy to compensate you," said the giller.

Kef glared at Gabine. "Let me handle this."

The old woman scowled and crossed her arms. "We could practically buy another boat with that."

"Not a good one," said the giller. "And not in this city."

"Sixty-five is fine," said Kef.

They paid the giller. The woman slipped the coins into a waterproof pocket. From another pocket, she handed Kef a small metal token.

"Give this to any guards that question you. It'll get you a berth in the port."

The giller walked to the bow. She paused, then turned back to Kef.

"A word of advice: I'd not stay long in Zorith, if you can manage it. Our new leader has yet to create the ... right kind of conditions for business."

Kef nodded. "Thanks for the warning."

The giller dove over the side, her body curving into a smooth bend as she sliced into the water. A faint ripple radiated through the inky black sea. Kef started the engine again. Their boat puttered towards Zorith.

"Nicely done," said Kef.

"Trust me, I've had far too much experience with negotiations. Sometimes it feels like I've spent half my life arguing with contractors."

Gabine looked in the drawer beside the steering wheel, where another eighty luras were hidden underneath a false bottom she'd rigged up. Kef had been planning to hide the coins in her underwear, knowing that they'd probably need bribes to enter. Gabine's idea had been far more elegant. Once a designer, always a designer.

"And the other half of your life?" Kef asked.

Gabine glowered. "Making mistakes."

"While we're on the topic, I should give you a warning." Kef swivelled in her chair to face Gabine. "Right now, you're thinking of all the ways you could run, or betray me to the guards, or maybe even just shove a harpoon in my back when I'm turned the wrong way."

Gabine opened her mouth to protest.

"It's alright," said Kef. "I don't take it personally. I've been in your place before. Just know this: I'm here to help you. Yes, we escaped Blackrake. But their guards? They'll be pissed. Not only did we escape execution, but we did it right in front of a crowd of honourborns. Embarrassing, eh? They're probably sending hunters out now and you don't have the skill to hide from them."

"And you do?"

"My skill goes beyond that. I've a task to do here, and once you've helped me do it, I'll set you up with a new identity and transport you to another city-ship. You can start afresh."

Gabine paused. "You do know why I was in Blackrake, right?"

"Yup. I read your file."

"You read my – of course." Gabine rubbed a finger on her left hand. "Fine. You know who put me there, and why. Do you really think they'll forget about it?"

"Nope. Gabine Wilfred-Jones Ruth will be hunted for the rest of her life. But if my mission goes to plan, by the end of the week you won't be Gabine. You'll have a new identity, a new history – shit, a new face if I can manage it."

Gabine snorted. "I could do with a new face. This one's getting old. Alright, I don't know how you'll manage that, but if you can break me out of Blackrake, then I suppose it's possible that you might pull this off, too."

Kef grinned. "Now that's the spirit."

As they neared the city, the hum of engines grew louder. Waves slapped harder against their hull. Kef noticed Gabine shivering. Kef didn't mind the cold, but she was still looking forward to getting inside Zorith's harbour. A storm was coming.

Kef led their vessel to a gap between the clustered boats. A wide opening led into a harbour housed within the city-ship's heart. Bodies hung from cranes. Victims of Exoran's coup, she presumed. Hundreds of cannons sprouted from the sides of ships and dozens of wingers circled through the air above. One blast from those cannons and their jetboat would be reduced to smoke.

A thick chain blocked the harbour's entrance. Kef raised her hand, holding the giller's token and hoping she hadn't been swindled. Light reflected off something from atop a tall observation tower at the mouth of the harbour. Kef squinted up. Was that someone with a telescope, looking down at her?

With a groan of metal, the great chain blocking the harbour lowered slowly into the water. Waves rippled out from the chain, bobbing their boat. Kef leaned on the wheel, waiting. Judging by the smell in the air, it would soon rain. Best they got into lodgings before then. When it stormed in Zorith, it was less like rain, and more like a tidal wave falling in the wrong direction.

After an eternity, the chain dropped. Kef gave a jaunty salute, then glided the speedboat into the harbour. The back of her neck itched. She didn't like how the surrounding ships loomed far above, or how spotlights roved across the water, fixing their blinding glare onto her craft. Squinting from the brightness, she almost crashed into a huge barge, and it was only a last-minute swerve that saved her. The captain swore and blew his horn. A pungent waft of Nanlimar Basin spices made Kef's eyes water as they passed.

"Good evening to you, too," she muttered.

They wound through the bustling harbour. Bottles and plastic floated in the oil-slicked water, bumping against their hull as they glided through. Bilge pumps spurted water out from the surrounding boats, splashing into the filthy sea. Combined with the city-ship's churning engines, they filled Kef's ears with a low-pitched rumbling that echoed off the huge tankers forming the harbour's walls. A dark smog wrapped around them: petrol-smoke, steam, and alchemical fumes, all forming into a hazy cloud of pollution.

As she approached the jetties, Kef frowned. There were plenty of free berths, but dozens of boats floated aimlessly in the middle of the harbour, attached to their own moorings.

"Why aren't they on the jetty?" asked Gabine.

"Maybe they tried to leave, but the harbourmasters stopped them. But they don't want to keep paying for jetty-spots, so they've made their own berths. Might be something to do with this new High Captain."

They reached the jetty. Kef lashed the boat in place, showing the giller's token to a frowning guard. He grunted, then walked away. Not exactly service with a smile, but she'd take it.

Thunder rumbled. Sprinkles of water fell onto Kef's skin, and then a moment later rain poured from the sky, drumming on the city's metal with a pounding intensity. Kef stuck out her tongue. The rain had a metal tang and tasted faintly acidic.

The wind changed, sending a fresh stench of sewage and butchered meat crawling up Kef's nostrils.

Gabine hunched over, gagging. "I forgot how good it smells."

Kef spat into the water, then jumped onto the jetty. "Ah, Zorith. Pleasant as always. Now, let's walk. It's time I explained our mission."

Chapter 4: A Vengeful Gaze

K ef slapped coins onto the counter. "Reservation for Kirsty, please."

Behind the bar, the innkeeper's pudgy hands dropped the coins into the pocket of his stained apron. He slapped two rusted keys onto the bar.

"Room three, as requested, madam."

Kef grunted thanks and took the keys. Located on level five of *The Lucky Robust*, the *Poor Canary* was barely large enough to be called an inn, with the common room occupied by a narrow bar and several stools running alongside it. Spiderwebs crowded the corners and rising damp stained the walls. Apart from Kef, Gabine, and the innkeeper, it was empty. This place didn't see much business.

The innkeeper opened a trapdoor behind the bar and climbed down into the darkness, clutching his money with one hand. Kef strode to the end of the crammed room, where a narrow stairwell led up to the second level. Anyone who wanted to reach her room had to climb these creaky stairs. She'd hear them a mile away.

Kef reached out to help Gabine up the steps, but the old woman shooed Kef away.

"I can manage," Gabine said, scowling.

Gabine did manage, but slowly, placing both feet onto the same step before moving to the next.

"You promised to tell me your plan," said Gabine, panting.

"When we're in the room," Kef said.

They emerged into a short corridor where rust coated the metal walls. Three doors lined one side, each leading to a room. Kef had reserved all three of them under different names, the week before entering Blackrake. She crouched beside the first door, inspecting it.

"What are you doing?" asked Gabine.

"I put a piece of clear tape across the door and the frame, right down the bottom. I've had these rooms reserved for two weeks with instructions that no one enters." Kef found the tape. "And no one has. Good."

Same for the second door. Nodding, Kef opened the third door, then stepped into their room. Nothing fancy, just two narrow beds with grimy blankets and battered storage trunks next to them. A faded light bulb illuminated the room with a sickly yellow light. Around the light bulb, the ceiling tiles sagged so much they looked in danger of falling, and flakes of dust hovered in the air. Kef made a mental note to keep her mouth shut while sleeping.

At the end of the room was a porthole, big enough to crawl through. Rain splattered against the dirty glass. The window looked out onto a tangled metal jungle of masts, rope bridges, and scaffolding, rendered into shadowy outlines from the streetlights. An immense tower rose from the city-ship's centre, dwarfing the surrounding vessels. A lightning bolt struck the tower's spire, bathing the city in a flickering blue glow. Seconds later, thunder rattled the porthole.

After shutting the door, Kef walked to the porthole and

pointed at the distant tower. "This is a city of lightning. I plan to steal its power."

Gabine frowned. "I don't understand."

She kept her face well composed. Not even the slightest twitch of her eyes or any other sign of nervousness. Impressive.

Kef studied the old woman. "Oh, I think you do."

She took off her boots, then stepped onto the nearest bed. It creaked. Kef pushed one of the ceiling tiles up out of the grid frame, exposing the cavity above. Dust billowed down onto her. She screwed her eyes shut, waving the dust away.

"What are you doing?" asked Gabine.

"You'll see."

The dust cleared, revealing the pipes and wires running through the cavity. Most of Zorith's big ships were built like this, with a drop ceiling hanging a foot or two beneath the true structural ceiling, allowing for plumbing, electricity, and ventilation. This cavity, however, held something more.

Kef groped in the darkness until her fingers clutched a strap. Grunting, she pulled on the strap, sending a large duffle bag sliding out from the ceiling to land on the bed with a jangling thump. Gabine's eyebrows rose.

Kef replaced the ceiling tile, then unzipped the bag. Folded inside were several alchemically treated clothes. The fabric dried within seconds of leaving the water, and also drew moisture from the skin to dry the wearer just as quickly. Far more expensive than regular clothes, but worth it for the convenience.

Kef pulled the clothes out of the bag. Hidden beneath were guns, knives, and bullets, along with a host of other weapons: blastpoint mines, grenades, knuckledusters, gun silencers, and more. Enough to outfit a small army. Or one very well-stocked warrior.

"You're prepared," said Gabine. "I assume you've stowed resources all around this city?"

"You don't sound surprised."

"I'm a fast learner."

Kef opened a side pocket. Coins were stuffed inside, filling the pocket to the brim. Gabine made a startled choking sound. Kef pulled out a bracelet made from a tattered cord, which she slipped around her wrist. The familiar roughness of the frayed cord made her muscles soften. Hadn't felt right, going almost a week without that bracelet. Once she'd secured it, she again reached into the pocket, sliding her fingers past the coins until she grabbed two brass telescopes buried beneath the money. Kef gave one to Gabine and kept the other for herself.

"Huh." Gabine looked down at the telescopes. "I used to have these."

Kef extended her telescope and raised it to the window. "Look at the Tower."

With a resigned grunt, Gabine copied her.

Through her telescope, Kef saw wingers flying around the cylindrical Tower. Cannons protruded from shutters in the side. At the top, high above any other point in the city, a great glass dome sparkled as rainwater washed down the side. Leading up through the dome to burst out from its apex, an immense metal spire stabbed into the air, reaching up towards the rumbling storm clouds.

Metal struts, chains, and ropes attached the structure to the neighbouring ships, which were all at least ninety feet away from the Tower. Only one entrance led into the tower itself:

a narrow metal walkway linked to a neighbouring battleship, swarming with soldiers.

As they watched, another lightning bolt struck the Tower's spire. Electricity fizzled down the metal, illuminating the glass dome from the inside. A few seconds later, the delayed boom of thunder crashed into Kef's ears.

Kef lowered her telescope. "That's the Lightning Tower. Every other city-ship is powered by prana oil. Not this place. This place uses lightning. That spire takes the electricity down into the compound, where the Channeler captures that energy, then distributes it to the city. There's backup prana oil generators all across Zorith, of course, but most of the time, this city's power comes from that Channeler, which draws the lightning to the spire. And I'm going to steal it."

Kef waited. Gabine's face remained blank. Kef's research was true, then – Gabine really was as calm under pressure as all her disgruntled contractors had claimed.

"Why?" asked Gabine, handing her telescope back to Kef.

"Money," Kef lied. "You won't believe how much my client's paying."

Gabine glanced at the coins shining from inside Kef's duffle bag. "You never mentioned an employer before."

"Of course not. I didn't trust you."

"And now you do?"

"Absolutely not. Don't take it personally, but I trust no one. Luckily, now you're in too deep and betraying me would damn yourself." Kef tilted her head to the side. "Still nothing? I'm impressed."

Gabine raised her eyebrows. "What in the Twisted Seas are you talking about?"

"The Lightning Tower. I expected more of a reaction,

45

considering you designed it."

Gabine turned away. Kef grinned. Finally, some sign that she'd rescued the right person! Even with her extensive research, she'd almost doubted whether Gabine was really who Kef thought she was.

The old woman sat on the bed with a creak of springs and ran a hand through her wispy grey hair. "It wasn't just me. We had a team."

"But you were their chief architect."

Gabine sighed. "Yes."

"You don't sound proud."

"I'd be prouder if they'd paid me. I was the greatest architect in this city, back when I was your age." Gabine gestured at the porthole. "Half those boats out there – I designed them. I was the talk of Zorith. When they asked me to make a tower that harnessed lightning from the sky … I thought it would be my masterpiece. Turned out to be my tragedy instead. They took my plans, they took my inventions, and when we'd finished, they exiled my family and I on some ridiculous safety charges. I had to spend the rest of my life renovating boats for people who could barely afford their own clothes. And the rare ones with money had no taste. The Lightning Tower has powered this city-ship for more than four decades, and what did I get?"

Gabine stared down at the dusty floor. In the sickly yellow light cast by the solitary lightbulb, deep shadows lined her wrinkled face.

"I thought you artists didn't care about the money," said Kef.

Gabine barked with laughter. "That's what they told me, too. I lost my entire business thanks to the Tower, and no one even knows I made it."

"People do know. They just happen to fall into two groups:

the people that threw you into Blackrake, and me."

Gabine removed her optics, wiping off the rain-droplets with her shirt. "Making the Tower didn't put me in Blackrake."

"I know."

Gabine glowered. "Is there anything you don't know?"

"Plenty. Like how to steal the Channeler."

"You're wasting your time. There's no way to break into the Tower, and even if you got in, you'd never take the Channeler. I never even saw it – they installed it after my exile. However, judging by the chamber we made for it, it's gigantic. One woman could never steal it."

Despite her bitterness, she spoke with a hint of pride. Gabine sat up straighter, her hunch gone, and gazed towards the Tower as lightning and rain danced around the spire.

"I know I can't steal it, not by myself." Kef smiled. "But who said I was doing it alone?"

Chapter 5: Bloodied Waters

In the water below, the mondoceros lunged towards the giller. The giller swept to the side, avoiding the creature's piercing horn while also slashing her trident along the beast's flank. The creature thrashed. His flailing tail knocked the giller out of the water and into the air.

Around Kef, the crowd roared. A man sitting in front of her stood, cheering. The giller splashed back into the water, but Kef couldn't see what happened next, because the man was blocking her view. Kef scowled. Normally, she'd yell at him to sit down. Not today. Today, she needed to keep a low profile.

"Sit down, you oaf!" shouted a woman behind Kef.

The man whirled around to glare at the woman. "Don't tell me what to do, bitch!"

He clambered over the benches. Beer slopped out of his cup to splatter over Kef and the other spectators in her row, who all groaned and cursed. She sighed. Why was it that some people weren't content just watching a fight, but had to start one themselves?

Someone pushed the man, sending him teetering backwards. He slipped on his spilled beer and then tumbled down the benches, knocking people aside with startled shouts. With a thud, he landed on the platform at the bottom of the floating bleachers. Groaning, he sat up. A security guard strode forward to drag him away.

The crowd around Kef glared at the retreating man as the guard pulled him out of sight – and then the giller's spear flew out of the water, trailing blood from its razor-sharp prongs. A roar rose from the other bleachers. Everyone turned back to the fight, forgetting about the interruption.

It was early morning on Shoresday. In Zorith, that meant one thing: the Naumachia. Kef sat in one of the floating bleachers arranged around the Flatwater – a rectangular clearing in the city-ship's heart. Thanks to the surrounding boats, the Flatwater contained a large expanse of relatively still water, protected from the waves slapping against the outer fringes of Zorith. Thousands of people crammed into the bleachers, chanting and roaring, betting and swearing, drinking and cheering, squinting in the bright morning sun and swelling with one voice split through thousands of mouths.

On the side opposite from Kef, Zorith's elite watched from the deck of a purple-hulled barge. That boat belonged to the Kazzia, who ran the Naumachia. Honourborns on that barge might've had silken canopies to shade them and far more elbow room than the people around Kef, but the wealthy yelled just as loud as the rest of them. Next to the boat's hull, at the water line, a dozen gillers perched on half-submerged benches. They were all strong and powerfully built, except for one scrawny kid who sat apart from the others.

An open-topped cage floated in the middle of the Flatwater, with the edge rising two feet above the surface. Big enough to hold a blue whale with room to turn, it currently held two creatures.

49

The first was a giller, desperately swimming towards one end. Eriss had won all nine of her previous Naumachias, though this was the first time Kef had seen her in person.

A mondoceros chased her. The creature was the size of a shark, with a horn longer than Kef's leg. Normally, the water would have been too dark to see through, but alchemical treatments and glow cubes attached under the cage made the water clear as glass.

The giller slammed into the end of the cage. An expectant hush fell over the crowd and everyone leaned forward, benches creaking under their weight. Would Eriss try to climb up and escape? From the purple-hulled boat, guards raised their rifles.

Eriss grew still. Her long hair fanned out in the water around her head. The giller's trident had been knocked away; now she was unarmed and trapped.

The mondoceros accelerated, lowering its horn to aim at the giller's chest. Moving like the water itself, Eriss twisted away and the horn sliced a thin line of blood along her side. Would've stung like shit, but it wasn't a killing blow.

The creature tried to follow her, but it was moving too fast. Carried forward by its momentum, the mondoceros crashed into the cage with a muffled clang and its horn passed through a gap in the bars. The metal rattled. The crowd roared.

Before the creature could free itself, Eriss wrapped her arms around the beast, hooked her feet through the bars, then yanked to the side. Levered between the metal, the mondoceros' horn snapped off. Kef couldn't hear the sickening crack of breaking bone, but judging by the creature's spasms, it must have hurt.

The mondoceros' frantic writhing almost threw the giller off. But she held on. Stretching out, Eriss grabbed the broken horn. Baring her teeth, the giller plunged the horn into the creature's side, clouding the water with blood.

She held on until the creature stopped spasming. Then she let go and the creature sunk, limp and lifeless. Cheers erupted from the crowd.

With a spray of water, the giller shot into the air, landing on the cage's edge. Her long webbed feet curled against the metal, supporting her as she stood, raising her arms into the air, baring her teeth. Might've been a grin. Might've been a snarl. Bloody water rolled down her swimsuit. Out of the water, she was towering. Immense. A lifetime of swimming made gillers tall and strong, but Eriss must've been seven feet tall and her shoulders were broader than a dock worker's.

The crowd stood and applauded. Whistles and horns echoed off nearby boats, adding to the din. Fireworks exploded into the sky above the Kazzia's purple-hulled barge, spectators tossed water-lily flowers at the giller, and one enthusiastic drunkard screamed, "Marry me, Eriss!"

Kef didn't join in with the cheering. Instead, she slipped out of the stands and nodded to herself. Eriss was good.

And by the hour's end, she'd be part of Kef's team.

Chapter 6: The Deal

Even from the outside, the raucous laughter and shrieking music coming from the Kazzia's barge was deafening. Kef stepped onto the pontoon floating behind the purple-hulled boat.

"I've got a business meeting with the Kazzia," she said to a guard.

The guard examined her. She'd broken into a tailor's earlier this morning to steal the kind of dress an upper-class merchant might wear. Hidden beneath the long skirt, she wore trousers in case she needed a fast escape.

He grunted. "You know the rules?"

"No going up to the honourborn deck, no touching the merchandise, and no weapons."

The guard nodded. "Go on. She's in a good mood."

Kef frowned. She?

The guard patted her down to check for weapons – Kef had nothing – then opened a hatch. Kef climbed through. Noise hit her like a wave, magnified and distorted and echoing off the inside of the metal hull. The room was a cavernous chamber, occupying almost the entire interior of the barge. There were people everywhere, holding drinks, laughing, and re-enacting Eriss' performance. Mostly merchants, judging by their clothes.

Spaced around the room, eight rectangular openings punched through the floor, each connected to an open-topped cage to create pools filled with sea creatures. Next to Kef, the water frothed with piranhas dismembering a seal carcass. A jellyfish floated in the next pool, changing colour with hypnotic pulses. Further along, a baby mondoceros butted against the edge of its cage. Someone had stuck an apricot on its horn.

Part zoo, part tavern, the Kazzia's barge was always alive and frenetic – but even more so after a Naumachia.

Kef wove through the crowd. She heard snatches of conversation as she wound past the well-dressed merchants.

"– that was nothing, you should've seen the leviathan we survived in the Deadcour Vastness –"

"– going to the High Captain's party tonight, I hear it's –"

"– can't be just me, oil reserves have never been this low –"

Something felt wrong. Was it her imagination, or did everyone seem tense? They might be laughing, clapping each other on the back, and smiling, but those smiles didn't reach their eyes and those laughs seemed forced.

Kef passed the largest pool, where Eriss, the other gillers, and a few regular humans rested on seats submerged a foot beneath the water's surface. A handful of colourful clownfish darted between them. Eriss had her arm around a man who sat next to her, wearing a suit jacket despite being in the water. The man said something and she chuckled. The others in the pool joined in, except for a scrawny giller sitting in the corner, whose shortness meant only his eyes were above the water. Or maybe he was just slouching.

Kef stepped between a slender woman wearing a shimmering gown and a man with alchemically dyed golden eyes. She emerged in a clearing. Ahead, the room narrowed to a triangle. Must've been at the end of the boat, right in the prow. Guards clustered around the edges of the clearing.

With their dark suits and thick necks, they stood out like stones in a pool of pearls. At the narrowest point of the boat, where the metal walls curved together into a sharp corner, a raised dais held a plush armchair. Emeralds studded into the furniture and an elaborate painting of Zorith's skyline hung behind the seat.

A stout woman lounged in the chair, with three Nanlimar Basiners perched on the edge of the dais. They talked to her in low, urgent voices. When she saw Kef looking at her, the woman in the chair raised her hand, silencing the Basiners.

"Can I help you?" asked the woman.

Her voice was deep and soothing. Just listening to her made Kef want to relax, which would be a mistake, because now all the surrounding guards were looking at her.

"I'm here for the Kazzia," said Kef.

The woman gestured to herself. Golden rings sparkled on her thick fingers. "You're looking at her."

Kef frowned. "What happened to Ornet?"

"Tragically, he is deceased." Judging by the cold gleam in the woman's eyes, she didn't think it was that tragic. "The poor fellow drowned in the riots following the High Captain's election."

Kef huffed. Couldn't the bastard have lasted another week? Damn it, Ornet had taken a month to agree to Kef's deal and securing his contract had been critical. She needed his asset to steal the Channeler. Would the new Kazzia honour his bargain?

54

The Basiners stood. With hurried bows to the Kazzia, they shuffled away. Around Kef, people went quiet and guards rested hands on their holstered guns. It clicked for her, then. During the chaos of the riots, this Kazzia had killed Ornet and taken his place.

If she thought Kef and Ornet were allies, she might suspect Kef was here for revenge. Maybe it was better to turn tail. There must've been twenty guards within a dozen paces, and every one of them was watching her.

Kef steeled herself. No, this was her only chance for breaking into the Tower. She couldn't back down.

"That's unfortunate," said Kef, adding a shrug to show she cared about Ornet as little as the new Kazzia did. "I had a deal with him – purely business, you understand. Although ... I don't suppose you'd accept the same offer?"

"What was your deal?"

"I need to hire a giller for a scavenging job." Kef pointed at Eriss, floating in the pool. "She'll do nicely."

"And what if they're not for hire?"

"Then I'll go somewhere else."

"There is no one else. I own all of Ornet's gillers. All the other ones in Zorith work for the guard."

"I suppose that's me out of options, then. Everyone knows the guard can't be corrupted."

The corner of the Kazzia's mouth twitched. Good. Kef was getting to her. Trying to corrupt a guard-owned giller would be more difficult, though, so Kef would rather avoid that.

"What was he charging you?" the woman asked.

Kef paused. Now would be a good time to lie.

"You already know," said Kef. "You've looked through his records."

The barest hint of surprise flickered across the woman's face, gone in an eye-blink. "What makes you think that?"

"I'm a good judge of people."

"Then perhaps you can tell me what I'm going to do next."

"One of two things. The first: you assume I'm lying about my intentions and I'm really here for revenge. In that case, you get the guard behind me to slide his knife in my back. He's already got the blade out."

A grunt came from behind Kef. "She's good."

Kef smirked. "Luckily, there's a second option. You know how much I was paying Ornet, so you take the contract, probably with some extra fee on top, and we haggle for a while before both walking away happy."

"I'm not walking anywhere. This is my boat."

"Figure of speech, ma'am."

The Kazzia gazed at Kef with cold eyes. Kef stared back, smiling. More people were watching her now, although they tried to hide their stares. This was bad. The Kazzia had the upper hand and Kef was surrounded on all sides. If a fight broke out, she'd never escape. Still, she forced herself to look relaxed. A lifetime of staring into danger and somehow surviving had given her the ability to always look confident, even if she didn't feel it. Especially when she didn't feel it.

"Triple your previous contract," said the Kazzia. "Ten thousand luras."

Gasps sounded around Kef. That was more than most merchants would make in a year.

"That's a little steep –"

"And half payment up front."

Kef paused. "That wasn't the deal I had with Ornet."

"I'm not Ornet."

"My client won't pay upfront. He's not even paying me until the job's done."

The Kazzia smiled coldly. "I trust you'll convince him otherwise, then."

"It would be much easier convincing him if you lowered the payment. Surely getting it early deserves some discount."

"That's fair. Nine and a half thousand."

"Eight."

"I hold all the leverage."

"So did Ornet, but that's the thing with levers. They can slip from your grip so easily."

"Nine and a half." The Kazzia leaned forward. "If you don't like it, go corrupt the guard. I'll be sure to attend your hanging."

Kef sighed. "Fine. Don't blame me when my client says no. Now, in terms of the giller in question, I'll pick –"

"You pay me first. Then you pick."

"Hang on, I don't see –"

"And you get me the money by this time tomorrow, or the deal is off."

Kef glowered. Her fingers were itching to curl into a fist, but she forced herself to take a deep breath, then smoothed a smile over her face. This was annoying. Between all her supply caches she'd hidden around Zorith, she had enough money to make her deal with Ornet work. But it wasn't anywhere close to the new Kazzia's demands.

She could try stealing Eriss, but then she'd have the Kazzia after her. No, for her plan to work, she had to keep a low profile. Starting a fight in here – with hundreds of people watching – wouldn't fit that plan. Unfortunately, that meant she'd have to eat the shit she'd been served.

"That won't be a problem," said Kef. "See you tomorrow."

Chapter 7: Perfect Delusions

Kef stormed into her room and slammed the door. She paced across the squeaky floorboards, then collapsed on the creaking bed.

Gabine sat on the other bed, drawing board in her lap, mechanical pencil in her hand. The old woman brushed a strand of grey hair away from her eyes.

She scowled at Kef. "You knocked my line."

Kef rolled over to look at the woman's half-drawn plan of the Lightning Tower. "Looks perfect to me."

Gabine returned to drawing. "I wish the same could be said for you."

"I could sink the Kazzia's boat like *that*, and that bitch thinks she can control me!"

"Is the boat still floating?"

Kef grunted.

"Then it appears she is indeed correct," said Gabine. "Let me guess. You were hiring a winger?"

"Giller."

"Might as well be the same. Mutant rental prices are ludicrous."

Kef rolled onto her back and stared at the ceiling. Why did she feel so listless?

"You've hired them before?" she asked.

The scratching of Gabine's pencil gliding across paper was oddly soothing. "I had to design an underwater military installation, about thirty-five years ago. I wanted to use regular builders for it, but the client insisted on hiring gillers. We told him they'd be more expensive, but he didn't believe us until we handed him the bill. That client never hired us again. Tried to sue us as well, would you believe it?"

"Some people want everything for nothing."

Gabine snorted. "When it comes to art, you can apply that label to just about every customer."

Groaning, the old woman stood, clutching onto the bed frame for support. She stuck the drawing to the wall, next to the other plans of the Lightning Tower. Gabine had made progress. None of those drawings had been there when Kef left in earlier this morning. That was good. They needed schematics for the heist. Can't scheme without schematics, as Plank used to say.

Damn, Kef felt tired. Not much sleep these last few days. Although what really worried her wasn't the sleep, or even the Kazzia's demands. What worried her was Zorith. The smells, the constant thunder, the guards puttering through waterways on their boats – she'd tried treating it like another job. For most of these first few days, she'd succeeded with that lie. But moments like these, where things were quiet and she had time to think … well, there'd be more action soon. Hopefully that would smother her worries.

Gabine came back to sit on the bed. It creaked. Or maybe that was her bones.

"So," The old woman clipped a new sheet of paper to her drawing board. "Did you get the giller?"

"No. My new contact needs half payment upfront."

"Ah. And I'm assuming you don't have it?"

"No."

She had to refocus. The minute, the hour, the day, the mission. Kef sat up. Blood drained from her head, making the room spin around her. She pulled jerky from her pocket. Popped it in her mouth. Chewed.

"But by midnight, I will." Kef gestured towards the porthole. "There's money for taking in this city, if you know where to look."

Gabine followed Kef's pointing finger. *"Flagship Augustine?"*

Amongst the thousands of boats that formed Zorith, *Augustine* was the largest. Floating shining and proud at the city's stern, its huge hull curved into the air, glowing with the freshness of new paint. A white beacon of radiance amongst the city's chaos. Ironic, really. It was the biggest ship in the city, yet held the fewest people. Maybe it needed the space to hold its passengers' enormous egos.

"I helped renovate that," said Gabine. "Scoundrels, the whole lot of them. You would think with so much money they'd pay on time."

"In my experience, that's why they have a lot of money in the first place."

Kef opened her bag and rifled through the clothes inside. The dress she'd stolen from the tailor's was suitable for acting as a merchant, but she'd need something even more exquisite to enter *Flagship Augustine*. Fortunately, she'd stolen several outfits from the tailor. He really should've installed a better lock.

Gabine turned back to her drawings, leaning close to erase a line. "So what? You're going to steal from the honourborns?"

60

"Nothing honourable about them. They're just given that title on account of living in the richest ship in the city."

"And one of the best protected."

"Granted." Kef found a glittering fascinator, bedecked with jewels that looked pricier than they really were. "But all the protection in the world won't stop me. I picked up some gossip on the way back. As luck would have it, they're holding a gala tonight to celebrate the reign of our glorious new High Captain Exoran. Being generous folk, they're inviting the best and brightest – out of the rest of us rabble – to attend. There'll be hundreds of other high-ranking citizens on *Flagship Augustine* tonight, along with all the honourborns who live there. I'll sneak aboard to see what I can filch. I'd imagine five thousands luras of jewellery would be easy enough to find, and with everyone distracted by sucking up to the new High Captain, it should give me the perfect cover. Good chance to see the new High Captain, too. Callaghan was … predictable. This new guy – I need to get a sense of him."

"Aren't there easier ways to get the money?" Gabine asked.

Kef smiled. She felt better now. She always felt better with a plan.

"Maybe," she said. "But nothing this fun."

Chapter 8: Amongst the Righteous

At the entrance to *Flagship Augustine*, an orchestra wailed. At least that's what it sounded like to Kef. As for everyone else milling around the deck of the *Meridian Cruiser*, waiting to enter *Flagship Augustine's* sally port, they were busy praising its resonant quavers. Whatever that meant. Kef thought it sounded like birds getting tortured.

She threaded through the crowd, her silky dress and fluttering two-tailed cape stealing more than a few glances from tuxedoed men. With a body muscled and toned from a life of sailing, she stood out amongst the waif-like honourborn women, but her difference only made her appear more striking.

Kef passed a woman in a peach-coloured dress, plucking her entrance ticket from her open handbag. Light fingers, a subtle nudge on the woman's other side to make her look the wrong direction, and then softly gliding away through the crowd. Just like Plank had taught her.

With a zing of bowstrings, the orchestra came to a screeching stop. The crowd clapped. Then some idiot tossed a handful of coins towards the musicians, forcing everyone else to copy him or risk looking stingy. Coins clattered onto metal with a pleasing jangle. Better than the music itself, Kef thought.

Pistons hissed as the sally port swung open. Warm light flooded out from *Flagship Augustine*, along with an orderly line of guards.

"Please present your passes as you enter!" called a guards, his voice rough and deep compared to the singsong voices of the crowd. "May our ships float forever."

"May our ships float forever," echoed the crowd.

The guards wore blue coats with a shimmering, pearly sheen, along with golden half-capes that hung from their left shoulders. Topping off the display, ornamental bronze helmets sat on their heads, with Zorith's crest stamped into the heavy metal.

The guests formed into a line. Kef positioned herself near the front, far away from the woman whose pass she'd stolen, who was jostling at the back of the queue. They shuffled through the port.

"I just don't see why these guards are necessary," said a stooped-over man behind Kef.

"They're for our protection, Jeffery," said the woman beside him. "We can't take any chances, not with these horrible riots going on."

Jeffery sniffed. "Those bottom-feeders wouldn't dare come to the stern."

Kef thought about the Lightning Tower. Her gloved hands clenched into fists. None of these arrogant bastards knew about the blood that oiled their decadent lives, and even if they did, they wouldn't care.

Kef reached the sally port. She showed her stolen pass to a guard. He nodded. Kef strode into the entrance hall, following the other guests as they glided towards the ship's stern.

It was several moments before she heard raised voices from

63

the crowd behind her.

"You don't understand!" said a woman. "I had my ticket; I'm an honoured guest – it must've blown away in the wind!"

Kef smiled, letting herself flow along through the ship, one with the crowd.

The passageway curled to the side as they emerged into the cavernous ballroom, where music floated through the air, coming from violinists on the mezzanine above. Chatter and high-pitched laughter added to the noise, while men and women twirled on the polished wooden dance floor.

Dotted around the room, crystalcoats glittered in the light. Crystalcoats were people afflicted by a rare mutation that slowly petrified their skin into a clear, diamond-hard substance. The mutation gave them incredible strength, but through the process of spreading it locked their limbs, making them stiff and rigid. With frequent doses of an alchemical serum, crystalcoats could live for decades. But if they didn't get regular treatments, the mutation would spread across them, eventually working deeper into their bodies to petrify their muscles, their lungs, their heart. Or it could spread across their face instead, locking their mouth shut and leading to a slow death by dehydration.

The crystalcoats in this room were long deceased. Their bodies had fully crystallised, providing a distorted, fractured view of the room behind them. Dancers weaved between the corpses, seemingly unconcerned. Sure, petrified crystalcoats looked more like ice sculptures than people, but Kef still found them unsettling. She hoped their families had been paid well in exchange for selling these bodies.

Perfumes and colognes thickened the air with a smell so strong it made Kef dizzy. Then there was the smell of food.

Rich scents made her salivate, all coming from a banquet spread across a table which replicated the shape of the Twisted Seas. Inky blue liquid swirled within the resin tabletop, cursed to rage forever within the alchemical creation.

The first time Kef had snuck into a party like this, she'd been shocked by the amount of food. Then she'd been disgusted. Nowadays, it didn't affect her much. The rich hoarded things they didn't use and kept food they didn't want, while the poor starved and struggled for the privilege of scraps. That was the way of the world. It made Kef angry at times, but she saw no point changing it. Take the world's burdens on your shoulders and it'll break you. Your own burdens are more than enough to manage. That's what Plank used to tell her. She sighed. Fourteen years gone to the waters, and the old man's words were still fresh in her ears.

A fork clinked against a glass. The violinists faded into respectful silence and the dancers came to a stop with a fluttering of dresses. No longer masked by the music, the sound of distant thunder cracked through the night sky whilst flashes of blue light stabbed through the portholes. A gentle patter of rain drummed against the ship's hull.

At the other end of the ship, where the ballroom narrowed to a point, a spindly man emerged onto the mezzanine balcony. On his jacket, hundreds of buttons caught the room's light, flashing spots of brightness into the crowd. Kef appreciated the glare. It meant she had an excuse to look away from the man's ridiculously curled and greased moustache.

"Friends!" His smile revealed overlarge teeth, polished to a white almost as bright as his buttons. "Good men and women of Zorith! We come here tonight for a most special celebration of our glorious new High Captain, Exoran the Honourable!

Ladies and gentlemen – please put your hands together!"

A smattering of applause sounded from the crowd. Standing near the back of the room, Kef joined in. She'd never seen Exoran before – never heard about him, for that matter. But she doubted the honourable part. In fact, she doubted there was even such a thing as an honourable man, and claiming such in your title only made Kef doubt the virtue all the more.

Behind the announcer, doors opened onto the mezzanine. A tall figure unfolded from the doorway, combat boots thumping on the balcony as he strode to the railing. High Captain Exoran surveyed the crowd – a hawk, deciding which rat to devour. As light fell upon him, it illuminated a long scar stretching across his cheek.

A horrible tightness constricted Kef's throat. She stumbled to the side, placing a column between her and the High Captain. Heat flushed her face. Next to her, some of the other guests frowned. She forced herself to take a deep breath, trying to calm her racing heartbeat. This couldn't be.

"Subjects of Zorith," Exoran said in a deep, low voice that seemed to rumble the walls themselves. "May our ships float forever."

"May our ships float forever," repeated the crowd.

His voice shattered her feeble denial. It was him. Kef had thought she was free of him forever, but here he was again. Her tormentor, back from the dead. Or likely never dead in the first place, because she'd been too busy escaping to be certain. Shit, it had been fifteen years! She'd thought that wound had scabbed over, but now that scab had torn away and the wound was fresh and painful as ever.

"We enter a new era," said Exoran. "Gone is the weak hand of High Captain Callaghan. Gone is the chaos and cowardice of her reign. The Twisted Seas are more dangerous than ever, and if we are to survive and prosper, we must strengthen our city. We must cleanse ourselves of the rabble that seek to erode our lives. We must protect ourselves from other city-ships that mean to destroy our way of life. Just yesterday, our scouts saw Prowlerak less than fifty miles away."

The crowd shifted uneasily. Prowlerak was another city-ship made from a long line of boats, all strung together to form a stretching snake of a city. It had the habit of encircling other smaller boats, boarding them, killing most of their population, then enslaving the rest and adding the defeated boat to the city's long chain of conquered ships.

"There is only one path forward," said Exoran. "One path where we might survive. The path of order. We must bring order to Zorith. This is why you have elected me your leader and I mean to deliver on that promise."

Kef's breathing grew sharp and shallow. She hadn't known this man as Exoran. When she was a kid, he'd been just another one of her nameless jailers – one of the torturers who had made her childhood miserable. Now he ruled Zorith. If she hadn't been so hurt by all the world's injustices, it might have made her cry. But she knew tears solved nothing. Only action did.

Kef had to leave the room. She had to leave before any more pains from the past got dredged up by Exoran's words. But she couldn't. She'd come here not just for the money, but to know more about this new High Captain. Besides, leaving halfway through his speech would draw too much attention.

"A new reign must come with new rulers," said Exoran. "Some of Callaghan's staff have continued to work with me, having proved that their loyalty to Zorith is greater than their loyalty to any man or woman. But, unfortunately, this has not been the case for all of the governors. Some were found still flying the flag of Callaghan's sinking ship. They have been stood down. We need new leaders to fill their roles. Leaders with the strength to lead our great city-ship through these troubling times. I hope that some of these leaders stand amongst you."

People exchanged glances and low murmurs of excitement circled throughout the room. Kef shook her head. These people were idiots. You'd think that knowing most of the former governors were dead would've quelled their interest in politics, but no. Tell them nine out of ten times they'd be doomed to death, and they'd assume they were the lucky exception.

"Tonight, those who wish to join my government should inform my assistants. In four days' time, on Starsday, we will reconvene at the Lightning Tower to announce the candidates best suited for bringing order to Zorith."

More excited babbling ran through the crowd.

"There's never been a gala at the Tower before!" said an elegant-looking woman next to Kef.

"It's a new era," said the young man beside her, who was dressed in a purple suit and gazed at Exoran with hungry eyes. "A new era, for new heroes."

With the constant booming of thunder, and the fact that it was the city's main source of power, the Lightning Tower wasn't the best place to dance and sample canapes. But perhaps Exoran wanted to show his power. It would be a good setting for that. From what Kef knew about the tower, the best place for a party like this would be the glass dome right at the top.

Kef stroked her chin. She'd have to check with Gabine, but

she assumed the dome was completely disconnected from the rooms containing the Channeler. Even if Kef snuck into that event, there was no way to get between the glass dome and the Channeler, or Exoran wouldn't have risked holding the event in the Tower. Still, Kef could see how this could play into her plans. Poetic, really. In trying to display his power, Exoran's ego would let Kef steal it from underneath his crooked nose. For once the world was aligning with Kef's dreams.

"I look forward to working with you." Exoran's deep voice echoed through the room. "For the glory of Zorith."

The crowd raised their glasses. Kef grabbed a flute from the nearest platter and joined in with the crowd.

"For the glory of Zorith!" they chanted.

"And for its death," she whispered.

Chapter 9: Levers

Slipping out of the ballroom was easy. After milling amongst the crowd for a few minutes following Exoran's speech, being careful to stay away from Exoran himself, she plastered her best drunken expression across her face, then asked a servant where the bathrooms were in a slurred voice.

The servant led her along a corridor. Kef felt sorry for the man. Catering to rich idiots would drain a person, and after what she was about to do, he'd probably get fired. She sighed. That was the way of the world, wasn't it? Scavengers fighting over scraps while the wealthy watched and laughed.

While they walked, Kef reached underneath her sleeve. Her fingers brushed against her bracelet. When she'd fled from her childhood prison, it was the only thing she'd taken with her. The only happiness she'd found in those dark years. But reminders of happiness could form their own types of pain, and this bracelet had caused its fair share over her life. There'd been times when she hadn't worn it. Times when she'd sworn and shouted because she thought someone had thrown it away. Times when she'd wanted to burn it. And then the most painful and liberating time of all, when she realised the bracelet didn't deserve to burn for her past. Zorith did.

The servant led Kef around the corner. With a bow, he pointed to the restroom.

Kef swayed. "Better not be … no one else in there."

"Pardon, ma'am?"

"No one else – *hick* – can hear me crap."

The servant didn't even blink. "I understand. Let me check for you, ma'am."

He knocked on the door, and when no one responded he shuffled inside.

"All clear, ma'am."

Kef glanced along the corridor. Laughter echoed from the distant ballroom, but no one was in sight.

She strode into the bathroom, shutting the door behind her. A waft of scented fragrance wormed up her nostrils, coming from the lavender bouquets hanging beside the sink. Kef gagged. Alchemically modified plants made her sick, but honourborns seemed to love them. Or maybe they just hated people smelling their shit.

The servant tried to scoot around her, eyes downcast, but before he could reach the door she slipped behind him, got the man in a chokehold, then covered his mouth with her free hand. He struggled, making muffled squeaking noises. Kef dragged him down to the ground.

"Calm down," she whispered in his ear. "I won't kill you."

As irony would have it, that made him struggle harder. Kef shook her head. There was no getting logic into some people.

She held the chokehold until his arms flopped onto the tiled floor. After a few extra seconds, just to be sure, she released the grip. Kef crossed the room, locking the door, then dragged him into one of the three cubicles, where she tore strips off his uniform to tie him to the railing. More torn strips formed a gag. It wouldn't do much to keep him quiet, once he woke, but hopefully they were far enough away from the party for no one to hear him.

Kef closed the cubicle door, then crossed to the back of the bathroom. A tiled mosaic showed a leviathan erupting from the waves. Not something Kef liked to look at while she shat – on account of more than a few near-death experiences with the species – but she supposed rich folk had strange tastes.

The maintenance hatch was right where Gabine said it would be. Kef pried it open, exposing a narrow cavity in the wall, filled with rumbling pipes. A damp, mouldy odour crawled out.

Kef squeezed into the wall. As Gabine had told her, this was one of several plumbing cavities that led through the ship. Wasn't the nicest place to crawl through, and certainly not the driest, but Kef had crawled through enough muck in her life to deal with it.

From inside the cavity, she closed the maintenance panel. Darkness. She hated tight spaces to start with, but darkness made them twice as bad. Luckily, she'd prepared. She took an alchemical light-cube out from her pocket, then shook the dice-shaped block. Pale blue light flared through the resin, illuminating the space. She clamped her teeth around the cube, then climbed down, using the pipes as footholds. Gabine said this place was big enough for inspections, but Kef still felt a horrible sense of the walls closing in to bump her elbows and legs as she shimmied down. Good thing she only had to climb three levels.

She descended one level, then two, judging the distance by the light shining through seams in the access panels. When she got three levels down, she stopped. Pressing her ear against the inside of the panel, she listened. During the gala, all the stairwells would have been blocked, and it was unlikely that anyone would wander around here when there was such an important event upstairs. Still, it paid to check.

Satisfied that she was alone, she opened the access panel, then stepped into an empty bathroom. She peeked out into the corridor. Empty.

Kef crept through the hallway, heading towards the stern. Plenty of rich apartments around here, of course, but she'd scoped out a target who lived further towards the ship's prow – the richer end.

As she walked, it staggered her how far apart these doors were spaced. On most middle-class ships, you'd see maybe nine feet between entrances. Here, there were stretches of sixty feet between doors, showing how much bigger these homes were.

She arrived at her target. Crouching, she reached up into her hair. By most standards it didn't look particularly elegant, but it had enough style to justify the pins and clips she'd used to fix her hair into elaborate curls.

Kef pulled out a L-shaped torque wrench disguised as a hairclip, and then removed one of her earrings, which was really a rake pin. She'd made it a year after Plank took her into the Sea Scars, and it had never let her down.

She slid the wrench into the bottom of the lock, applying a slight clockwise pressure, then wriggled her rake pick into the mechanism, scrubbing it against the pins inside. Her fingers responded to the cylinders' movement, feeling the pins push up in response to her rake, feeling the pressure ease on her torque wrench. The lock clicked. After replacing the tools back into her hair, she stepped inside the room.

Kef had expected opulence, but the scale of the room still surprised her. It was a two-story affair, with a glittering chandelier hanging from the ceiling. Plush couches dotted around the space. They looked untouched. Artworks and sculptures littered the sumptuous space, with more doors leading off to other rooms. At the far end, a wide glass door led onto a private balcony. Soft music played from an elaborately curved gramophone and the scent of lavender wafted up Kef's nostrils.

She strode towards the drawers. Those artworks would be more than pricey enough, but she needed things that were easier to carry. She ripped drawers out of cupboards, letting glasses and silken clothes and letters tumble onto the carpet. Took a few goes, but eventually she found a pearl necklace. She frowned at the beads. Looked genuine enough – that was probably a few thousand luras right there, with the right fencer.

Last time she'd been in Zorith, she'd staked out this room's owner, who was one of the richest women in the city. She'd been planning a more elaborate con for the future, but fleecing her now felt just as satisfying.

She heard a click.

Kef looked up to see the door handle turning. She cursed. It had been locked – she was sure of it. Before she could move, the door flung open and a man wearing an extravagant purple suit strutted inside, holding the hand of a giggling woman behind him.

"Here, my lady, I think we will be quite –"

He froze, gaping at Kef. The woman bumped into him, almost knocking him over. She saw Kef. Her giggling turned into a squeak, and then her face paled as she stumbled out of the room, muttering how this wasn't a good idea. The door slammed shut behind her.

Kef sighed, then strode towards the man. She didn't have a knife but wouldn't need one to deal with this.

He raised a trembling hand. "Halt, my lady! One more step and I'll call the guards!"

Kef stopped walking. "Wouldn't advise that. Do you know why I'm here?"

He surveyed the room, observing the clothes strewn across the floor, the drawers flung open, and the jewellery scattered across the rich carpet.

"To – to thieve!" the man said. "From your rightful betters –"

"Do you know whose room this is?"

"Of course. It belongs to Ruby Starletta, director of the cargo guild." The man gulped. "My great-aunt."

That would explain why he'd been able to unlock the door.

"Lots of people want her job." Kef patted a mondoceros-ivory table. "Lots of people probably want this room, too."

The man's eyes narrowed. "I – I sense that you're encircling around the truth. Would it not be best to speak it directly?"

"I work for High Captain Exoran's intelligence team. We've heard Starletta's still sympathetic to the old High Captain, that she's working on staging a coup. Might be a load of dung. Might hold some truth. Either way, Exoran told me to dig through her stuff, see what I can find."

His face paled. "Why are you telling me this?"

"First – so you don't do anything stupid, like calling the guards or leaving this room. Wouldn't be bad for me, since I'd just escape, but you might find yourself wearing some concrete boots."

"C-concrete boots?"

"We set your feet in a bucket of concrete, then toss you into the sea."

He gulped. "I'm s-sorry. I didn't realise – p-please, I swear I won't tell anyone."

Kef pointed at a chair. "Sit."

He collapsed into it, shaking. "P-please don't kill me."

Funny, how quickly a posturing fool could become a whimpering mess. Killing him made sense. She could probably do it quietly and quickly enough that no one else would hear. Kef stroked her chin. No … perhaps she could make use of him instead.

"Tell you what." Kef crouched down to match his eye level. "What's your name?"

"N-Nicholas." He swallowed. "Nicholas Patrick Bartholomew the Second."

Kef cringed. "Can I just call you Nick?"

He nodded, golden hair flopping against his forehead.

"Nick. We're always looking for more hands, in my line of work, and it seems you're well-placed to be a valuable asset. How would you feel about working for me? Times are turbulent, and it's not a job for everyone, but if you came back with some good reporting, something that might help us uncover traitors … why, I wouldn't be surprised if Exoran found a spot for you in his new government. What do you reckon?"

Even before she finished, she knew his answer. The fear was probably enough to make him agree, but she'd sensed something else that would gain his commitment more firmly than the deepest fear. Greed. He was a courtier, an aspiring member of Zorith's upper class. And he'd do anything to claw his way higher.

"I'll do it!" He puffed out his chest, drawing Kef's attention to the ridiculous ribbons flopping down from his shoulder-pads. "I'll be the greatest spy you've ever known!"

"Spies aren't supposed to be known."

"Oh." His chest deflated a little. "Then – I'll be the greatest spy *never* known!"

She slapped his knee. "Good man."

Crossing to the desk, she grabbed a pen, then scrawled an address on a scrap of paper, which she tossed to Nicholas.

"Any information you get, send it there, addressed to K. That's me. Use a different courier each time – and never yourself."

"I understand, madam! I will be excellent at this task, for I have extensive experience in communications and supply chains –"

"I'm sure you do. Now go find that woman of yours and make sure she doesn't talk."

He leapt up, puffing his chest out once more. "As you command, madam! She is – er – unlikely to talk about this, anyway, as she is still technically courting … uh, never mind. But by the winds of the sea, I shall ensure it!"

"May our ships float forever."

"May our ships float forever!"

The man pranced out of the room. When the door shut, Kef stared at it for a long moment, scarcely believing what just happened.

She gathered the most expensive-looking jewellery and shoved them into her pockets, not caring about the mess she left behind. Then she opened the sliding glass door, stepping out onto the private balcony.

Cold wind chilled her skin and a smattering of rain pissed through the open door and onto the carpet. Thunder rumbled as a bolt struck the Lightning Tower. She took a deep breath, savouring the scent of the storm. Then she dove off the balcony, falling away from the ship's curving hull, her dress fluttering in the air, diving into the dark water.

THE KAZZIA PRESENTS ...

★ ★ ★ ★ ★ ★ THE ★ ★ ★ ★ ★ ★

28TH NAUMACHIA
OF THE YEAR 781 AC

★ ★ ★ ★ ★ ★ ★ ★ ★ ★ ★ ★ ★ ★

ERISS VS LANCE
THE GILLER   THE MONDOCEROS

DIRECT ALL BETS TO SACH & RELET BOOKEEPERS

SHORESDAY MORNING · THE FLATWATER

Chapter 10: No Such Thing

K ef tossed a sack of coins onto the floor. "Here's your money, Kazzia."

The Kazzia reclined on a soft velvet lounge. She didn't look away from the waters below, where her gillers were swimming laps in the Naumachia cage. A guard picked up the sack of coins and started counting.

The Kazzia turned to stare at Kef. They were on the top deck of her purple-hulled barge, shaded by canopies stretched overhead. Anyone lesser than a honourborn couldn't come up here during a Naumachia, but with no events on, the only people here were the Kazzia, servants cleaning the deck, and her guards. And there were a lot of the latter. Too many for Kef's liking.

The Kazzia took a medallion from her pocket, then flipped it over and over between her stubby fingers. The dark metal seemed to suck in the light. Kef's eyes narrowed. Ruskar Steel. Stronger than any metal in existence, and with a price to match, its only source was skyfalls from the Debris Ring that orbited the planet. If the Kazzia wanted to flaunt her wealth, she'd picked the right prop for the task.

"I must say, I'm impressed with your client," she said. "Not all backers are so forthcoming with funds."

"I only work for the best."

"It seems that way."

A few guards grunted and shuffled away. Was it Kef's imagination, or did they seem disappointed, like they'd been robbed of a show? Could be the case. Fronting over four thousand luras was no easy task, and they never would have expected Kef to find the funds. She smiled. It always felt sweet to disappoint her doubters.

"Alright," said Kef. "Now for my giller."

She strode to the railing. Down in the water, the gillers were balanced on planks running from one side of the cage to the other, with the water lapping right beneath them. All the gillers fought one-on-one with short wooden poles, except for the woman on the middle plank. That was Eriss, who'd killed a mondoceros in yesterday's Naumachia.

She duelled against two gillers coming at her from either side. One was a woman and the other was a man, and both looked like children compared to her. The man swung at her head with his pole as the woman lashed at Eriss' ankle. Eriss let the stick crack into her ankle without so much as a wince, and grabbed the man's pole with her huge webbed hand. She wrenched the pole sideways, sending the man splashing into the water, then twisted around, using the momentum to slam the man's pole against the other woman. A loud crack echoed across the water. The impact slapped the woman into the sea, joining the other man.

Kef nodded. Most gillers were clumsy out of the water, especially big, seven-foot tall ones like Eriss. But her balance and timing was perfect.

Eriss reached down to help the other gillers climb up onto the plank. Neither looked angry. They just seemed resigned, like they'd expected her to win.

Kef pointed at Eriss. "That one."

"No," said the Kazzia. "This one."

Guards emerged from a door, followed by a skinny giller who barely came up to their shoulders. His yellow eyes flicked to either side and he hunched over even lower when he saw Kef. The kid looked like he'd barely gone through puberty.

Kef scowled. "Kazzia, we had a deal –"

"The deal was for a giller. Since you never specified which one, Squine will be perfectly adequate. Eriss is my biggest attraction. If you want her, it'll cost another five thousand."

Water dripped off the boy's swimsuit. He hugged himself and looked down at the deck, swallowing. A tattoo of the Asadi mark stretched across his throat.

"You can't be serious," Kef said. "This kid barely has scales."

"We did only get him last month."

Guards smirked at Kef. The Kazzia smiled at them with an indulgent expression. Kef scowled. No time to argue, but she wouldn't forget it.

"Fine."

A scribe came forward to slap papers into Kef's hand. "This is our standard rental contract."

"I've hired gillers before," said Kef through gritted teeth. "I know how their contracts work."

"Nevertheless, I must go through it. You have full control over Squine until midnight next Seasday. Any damages will incur additional expenses, in accordance with this section of the contract." The scribe pointed to the relevant clauses in the document. "Your giller has received the proper training and conditioning from the Asadi Institute, and will respond to and obey all your commands, except for those acting directly against the Kazzia. As per his conditioning, he requires one pill of Zetamyre each day, ideally first thing in the morning."

She produced a small metal canister with a combination lock built into it. Inside the canister, pills rattled as she handed it to Kef. Kef's eye twitched. She shoved the canister into a pocket.

"Failure to give him Zetamyre on the required schedule will result in severe withdrawals. This is as per his conditioning, to ensure he follows your orders absolutely."

Kef grunted. "If the giller annoys me, those drugs will be the last thing he'll need to worry about."

Squine hunched even smaller. The wind changed direction and Kef inhaled a mouthful of his odour: spilled oil, fish guts, sewage. Most gillers didn't smell this foul, but Zorith's pollution had clearly sunk into Squine's skin.

"The combination for the Zetamyre canister is contained in this envelope." The assistant gave it to Kef. "Your Writ of Lease is also in there. Any questions?"

"This is a giller, isn't it? Not some kid you fished from the sea?"

The Kazzia chuckled. "You get what you pay for, my friend, and this is all you can afford."

A guard shoved Squine in the back. The boy stumbled towards Kef, his bare feet slapping against the deck.

Kef sighed. "Wish I could say it's been a pleasure doing business."

The Kazzia smiled coldly. "When is business ever pleasurable?"

"Fair point." Still scowling, she nodded at the giller. "Come on, kid."

Squine stared at the gillers in the water below. A few were watching the proceedings with interest. Squine raised his hand to wave goodbye, but the other gillers turned away, laughing. The boy's face hardened. Kef strode towards the stern, and the boy stooped even lower as he stumbled behind her, dripping a path of water all the way across the deck.

#

Squine walked slowly. Too slow.

As Kef led him along a decrepit jetty, her boots splashed through puddles and Squine's bare feet slapped against the wood. She glanced back at him. The kid was staring at a small metal object in his hand. A locket?

"What's your depth rating?" she asked.

Squine looked up, startled. He shoved the locket into a pouch.

"Two hundred feet," he said in a soft, quivering voice.

Kef snorted. "I know humans who can dive that low. What about your sight range?"

"Fifty feet in the test, master."

"Damn, did you even train at the Institute, or did they just ship you out as soon as they got you?"

Squine made a choked mumble.

They stepped onto a large pontoon walled in by barges on either side, framing the grey sky above. Clotheslines stretched between the boats. A group of men sat on low stools, playing cards. When one of them saw Squine, his eyes widened.

"Hey, it's that giller!"

"Quit delaying, Nikos, you know I'm going to win this hand."

"No, look!" another man joined Nikos, pointing at Squine. "That's the little bitch that lost us our bet."

Squine's face paled.

Kef raised her hands. "Guys, I don't know what your gripe is, but we're not looking for trouble. Just passing through."

85

The men stumbled up, closing off the front and back of the rectangular pontoon to block the exits. Squine pressed against Kef's side. He was cold and wet. Kef elbowed him away, scowling.

"Wait," she said. "How do you know who this is? All gillers look the same."

They didn't, but Kef thought that line might work.

"Bullshit," said Nikos. "All them other ones are big and strong. This boy's a little worm. Three to one odds, this kid against a dolphin. No fangs, no spikes, and the little bitch crawled out of the cage the second the contest started."

"Kazzia should've shot him," growled another man.

"She would have if everyone hadn't laughed so hard," said Nikos, brandishing his half-empty bottle at Squine.

"Alright, you lost a bet," said Kef. "Boo hoo. Now get out of my way."

Nikos strode forward, leering. "I don't think so. We're going to teach this giller a lesson."

"I doubt it," said Kef.

She sucker-punched Nikos, knuckles cracking against his chin. He collapsed onto the pontoon in a tangle of limbs, and the bottle rolled out from his fingers. Kef grabbed it, then drank.

"Urgh." She dropped the bottle, which shattered. "I can see why you're in a bad mood."

Before anyone else could react, she drew a gun from underneath her jacket. She hadn't been able to take it onto the Kazzia's boat, but she'd hidden it under a nearby pontoon before climbing aboard. Around her, Nikos' friends stumbled back, yelping.

"We can all agree that a bet isn't worth getting shot for, is it?" she asked.

They nodded. Beneath Kef, Nikos groaned.

"Excellent. Now get out of my way."

Everyone pressed against the boats on either side of the pontoon, clearing the exit. Taking care not to rush, Kef dragged Squine away. When they'd put some distance between them and Nikos' friends, Kef put her gun back into the holster.

"Alright, Squine, time for swimming."

The kid kept staring down at the jetty beneath them. His fingers trembled.

Kef snapped her fingers in front of his eyes. "Kid. Swim time."

Squine flinched, startled. "S-sorry, master."

On the sides of his neck, his gills fluttered. Poor kid was nervous. Was he shaken from Nikos' words, or from something else? From her, maybe?

"You know your way around Zorith?" she asked, trying to soften her voice.

Squine nodded. "The Kazzia made us memorise maps."

"Good. Take me to the sternwards side of the Half-Flood Plaza. Come up every twenty seconds for air. Got it?"

He nodded. "I ... understand."

Kef put on her goggles, then grabbed the strap stitched onto the back of Squine's swimsuit. They dove into the chilling water. Squinting through the murky darkness, she adjusted position, wrapping both hands around the strap. The boy twisted to look at her. Surrounded by the yellow of his eyes, his slitted pupils were wide, giving him the ability to see further than she could. She nodded.

They shot into the darkness. Shadow and light blurred around them. Far down on the ocean bed below, faint pinpricks of illumination broke up the blackness. Those would be alchemical glow lamps, way down in the seaweed mines.

Water streamed Kef's hair out behind her as Squine swum, his webbed hands and feet propelling him through water, smooth as oil. Pressure built in Kef's ears as Squine dove under a barnacle-encrusted hull, then skirted around a rusted anchor drifting on the end of a short chain connected to a boat's prow. It'd been a long time since that anchor kissed the seabed. Maybe never. City-ships like Zorith stayed over deep water, roving across the waves, keeping a healthy distance from the monster-infested land that surrounded the Twisted Seas.

A deeper blackness pressed upon Kef as Squine shot under a cargo hauler. He wove through a maze of pipes sticking from the ship's underbelly. A burst of heat hit Kef as they passed one pipe. Probably some exhaust exchange. The water chilled again as they circled around a cage crammed with twisting fish and lit by a single flickering bulb. Kef smiled grimly. Hardly anyone from the city above looked beneath the surface of the seas, but most of what kept Zorith alive was down here, down in the cold and the dark.

Squine dragged Kef out from the boat's shadow and they floated upwards. Kef's ears popped as the pressure eased. They broke through the surface and Kef inhaled air, calmly, through her nose. She'd had plenty of experience free diving – anyone worth their salt in the Twisted Seas could say the same – and she could've held her breath far longer, but she was glad the boy had surfaced right on cue. That spoke well for him sticking to her future plans.

When she'd recovered her breath, Kef nodded. They plunged underwater again, diving into the depths, swimming through the dark jumble of boat-hulls and chains and debris. Kef found it strangely peaceful. Just the chill of the water against her skin and the muted softness of distant machinery. You didn't realise how noisy the city was until the sound went away.

After another six repetitions, the hulls grew larger, and began to be spaced further apart. They'd left the slums. Squine and Kef surfaced near an empty jetty on the sternwards side of the Half-Flood Plaza – a collection of rectangular pontoons, all joined together to form a flat, floating square several hundred feet in both directions. The jetty was one of a dozen small jetties sprouting out either side from a boardwalk that connected to the Half-Flood Plaza. Dinghies and glum-looking gondolas lined the jetties on one side. Squarish boat-restaurants were docked to the other – a big strip of them running along the boardwalk, painted garishly bright and bearing questionable signs boasting about their culinary prowess, like peacock-fish trying to outdo each other.

She strode towards *Raffe's Noodle Emporium.* An impressive-sounding name, considering how small and dirty this house-boat looked, sandwiched between two bigger barges that actually had customers. Or maybe *Raffe's* did have customers. Too much grime coated the windows for Kef to tell.

As she walked, her alchemically treated clothes wicked water from her skin. By the time she reached *Raffe's*, both the fabric and her skin were dry. Water still dripped from Squine's swimsuit, but that was less of an issue, since gillers didn't feel the cold.

A narrow plank joined *Raffe's* to the boardwalk, held in place with frayed ropes. When Kef stepped onto the plank, it creaked loud enough that she winced, but she got onto the deck without the wood snapping.

She glanced back. Squine stood on the boardwalk, hunched over in the shadow of a support post, like he was trying to hide. People sped up as they walked past, glaring at him. Most people preferred gillers to be submerged and not seen.

"Come on," she said. "The plank's fine. I'm heavier than you."

Swallowing, the boy pointed. "I can't. The sign."

A crude sign was nailed to the boat – a fish, with a red cross slapped on top of it: *No Gillers Allowed!*

Kef ripped the sign off. It splashed into the water.

"I don't see a sign," she said. "Come on."

Squine gaped. The expression made him look even younger, and he already looked like a kid. He stepped across the plank to join her, wood creaking beneath him.

Kef picked her way across the back deck. Crayfish pots and busted fishing rods littered the ground, along with droppings of seagull crap and dark oil stains. Just what you wanted outside a restaurant.

The door squeaked as Kef opened it to enter the diner. Inside, a bench divided the room in half. Five empty barstools stood on her side. A tiny kitchen occupied the other side, reeking of sweat and frying oil, although maybe that was just the natural smell of the scowling, monobrowed man standing behind the bench. He looked up from the glass he was dirtying with a blackened rag.

"Ain't open until –" His eyes widened. "Kef! It's – it's so good to see you."

Kef eyed the nearest barstool. Fifty-fifty as to whether it would hold her weight. She stayed standing.

"Likewise," she said. "Got my money?"

"Ah …" He gulped. "I –"

90

"Don't bother with the bullshit, Raffe. Get me a free lunch and I'll take off three luras."

"Lunch costs four," he said in a small voice.

Kef slapped her gun onto the bench with a dull clang.

"I'll get it right away!" Raffe said.

Squine stepped out from behind Kef. Raffe made a startled squeak and his face reddened.

"No gillers!" said Raffe, jowls quivering.

"He's with me," said Kef.

"Kef, you know why I don't … what happened, with my …"

Kef sat, gesturing for Squine to do the same. "That's got less to do with gillers and more to do with you. Get him whatever you're making me and I'll take another three luras off your debt."

Raffe's hands clenched into fists. Then he took a deep breath and turned to the kitchen.

Within minutes, two bowls of steaming yolk-noodles sat on the counter before Kef and Squine. Battered chopsticks protruded from them and flakes of dried seaweed garnished the dishes. Kef ate with relish. Hygiene wasn't Raffe's strong suit, nor cleanliness, nor customer service for that matter. But say one thing for the man – he cooked damn fine noodles.

Behind the counter, Raffe gnawed his fingernails. His gaze shifted from Kef to the rack of knives in the kitchen, then back to his grubby bare feet.

His double chin wobbled. "Are you going to kill me?"

Kef slurped a long noodle into her mouth, then tilted her head to the side. "Maybe if these stank. Lucky for you, they're as good as ever. You should be cooking for an honourborn."

Raffe hunched. You wouldn't have thought such a large man could look so small, but he managed it well. Funny, really.

91

People always thought looking small would save you from trouble. In Kef's experience, it usually brought it on.

"I'll pay you back soon," he said. "I haven't forgotten what you did for me, and – and – it's just … business has been slow, no one wants to eat in this part of town after the riots, and everyone's worried about Exoran –"

She waved a hand, still slurping noodles. "Relax. You'll pay me when you pay me. I'm not here for my money. For now, I'm just here for lunch."

She burped. Hmm. Maybe she needed to slow down on the noodles.

"Beer?" she asked.

Raffe practically hurled it at her. Kef chuckled, prying open the bottle. Tasted odd. Warm, too. Still, she wasn't picky when it came to booze.

Kef glanced at Squine. The boy's food was untouched. He hunched over the bowl, glancing at Kef with wide yellow eyes. She recognised his wariness. When Kef was his age, she'd always worried about gifts that seemed too good to be true.

She gestured at the noodles. "Go on."

Leaning low over the bowl, like he was trying to hide it, Squine used the chopsticks to carefully pull the noodles into his mouth. He ate in small, quick bites.

"Good eh?" asked Kef.

Squine nodded. "Thank you, master."

Raffe scowled down at the boy. "What do you normally eat?"

"Fish, sir."

"So you're cannibals, then?"

"So you're an arsehole, then?" asked Kef. "Let the kid eat. Go clean a plate or something. They bloody well need it."

Raffe's face twitched. He spun around, then stormed into

the kitchen.

"Good feed?" Kef asked Squine.

"Yes." Squine bobbed his head in a nod. "Thank you."

"Eat plenty. You've got a lot of swimming ahead of you."

That swimming would've been easier with Eriss, or one of the other, stronger-looking gillers, but hopefully Squine would be capable enough. Although given how skinny and small he was, he wouldn't be much good in a fight, if it came to that.

Not for the first time, Kef wondered if she should have used her regular crew. The Sea Scars were the closest thing to family she had in this world. After Plank's death had passed the captaincy onto her, she'd built the Sea Scars into a team just as talented at piracy as they were at slaying monsters.

Pidge could wrangle just about any creature into helping them. Ornery seemed to have memorised half the books that'd ever been written, and was smart enough to actually use that knowledge to free the crew from more tight spots than Kef could count. Waylon was one of the best-flying wingers in the Twisted Seas – and damn, the cocky little bastard knew it. Then, of course, was Treel. She was the strongest giller Kef had ever known. Far more competent than Squine and even better than Eriss, the giller from the Naumachia. And beyond that, she'd been Kef's best friend for half her life.

The Sea Scars would've helped her. But stealing from the Lightning Tower wasn't like other missions. When Kef told the Sea Scars she needed a few months on her own, they'd been confused. Frustrated. Especially since it came just after the shit-show of a mission that killed Laila.

A lump formed in Kef's throat. Laila used to be the crew's other winger. Despite her being just as competitive as Waylon, they'd balanced each other out surprisingly well, especially after Treel encouraged them to finally admit how they felt about each other.

Kef sighed. She tried not to think too much about Laila's death. Remember the rise, not the fall, like Plank had always said.

Treel, Pidge, Waylon, and Ornery – they'd wanted to help Kef, but she hadn't shared her plans, hadn't even said she was returning to Zorith. This mission had to be solved by herself, even if it made things harder. Even if it pushed away her friends.

"Master?" Squine asked. "Why are you doing this?"

"What, the job?" Kef finished her own noodles with a slurp. "Fine money in it, that's why."

"No." Squine pointed down at the noodles. "I meant this."

Kef paused. "Got something against noodles?"

Squine shook his head.

"Then I don't see why you're worrying."

Squine bowed. "I'm sorry, master. I didn't mean to offend you."

"You haven't. Just keep eating. We need to leave soon."

Kef watched as Squine ate. There were hard-headed reasons for giving him a decent feed, of course. He had a lot of tough work ahead. And Kef always found that the way to loyalty was as often through the stomach as through the purse. But she knew that wasn't her only motive.

Was this how Plank felt when he'd found Kef? A little girl, alone and terrified, so stupid she didn't know port from starboard or the sharp end of a knife from its handle. But he'd seen something in her. Taken her in as his apprentice. And even though he'd spent half his days cursing her incompetence, he'd been proud of her, in the end.

Out through the window, in the distance, when the rolling of the waters made ships sway the right way, she could glimpse *Flagship Augustine's* bridge. Exoran would be up there, most likely. Watching over a city terrified by his shadow, watching over everyone scrambling to prove their loyalty to him.

Kef scratched the pale spot on the back of her left hand. She'd managed to ignore her childhood for the best part of fifteen years, but now those memories were too painful to ignore. There was only one path to peace, and it was to rip out Zorith's heart.

She looked back at her food, twirled noodles around her chopsticks, then shovelled them into her mouth. Guess that's what it came down to. Not wanting to be like them. Trouble was, when you wrestled a man covered in filth it was hard to keep yourself clean.

Squine finished the last of the noodles. He wiped his lips with the back of his hand, then placed the chopsticks neatly beside each other on the bowl, exactly down the middle. Kef smirked. Either the boy thought he was some kind of mannered gentleman, or the Kazzia had spent way more time training gillers in table etiquette than was necessary.

"Alright." Kef stood. "Time to go. And Raffe!"

Raffe glanced up from the pipe he was lighting. "What?"

"Don't let this place sink before you pay me back." Kef strode out the door. "I'd hate to eat anywhere else!"

Chapter 11: Actions ...

Even on rare days where Zorith's sky was cloudless and blue, there was a draining greyness to the Alchemical Factory. Moored beside the desalination plant, the Factory loomed large amongst a teaming mess of smaller boats. Hulking and windowless, pipes and exhaust vents lined the hull, crawling down into the water like fungus sprouting from a mangy coat. Rifle-bearing guards strode along the deck, glaring down at any passers-by clueless enough to stop. Wingers circled above the ship, occasionally landing on observation towers for brief respites. From where Kef perched on a nearby boat mast, she guessed that gillers would be patrolling beneath the water as well.

All that security was there for a reason. Zorith wasn't as reliant on Alchemists as other cities were, since most of Zorith's power came from lightning, instead of extracting prana oil from seaweed. Still, Alchemists were crucial for turning raw minerals into useable goods that kept the city alive. They ran Zorith's desalination plant, too. For her part, Kef found most them annoying; too smug and uppity about earning their keep with brains instead of brawn. Still, there were good ones among them. She'd be meeting one of those today.

Climbing down from her perch, she picked her way across a jumble of shaky jetties, keeping her well-tailored pants out of the water as she wound between close-pressed boats to head towards the Factory's entrance.

Kef wondered again if she should have brought Gabine. It would've been easy enough. After dropping Squine back at the inn, in a special room made for gillers – with a bath to keep their gills moist – she'd checked in on the old woman. Gabine had been locked in her room, sketching plans on huge paper rolls. Seemed happy enough, with a pencil and T-square in hand. Kef had left her there. Maybe that was the wrong move. The old woman was a liability if things got heated, but she had also a cantankerous quality that was disarmingly respectable. Fine, classy manner about her speech, too. Good for mingling with the upper echelons, which was how Kef had planned to deploy her, but now that she had Nicholas Patrick Bartholomew, she might not need to.

She still couldn't get over meeting Nicholas on *Flagship Augustine*. He'd been practically begging to work for her, convinced that she'd deliver his hopes and dreams without the inconvenience of working for them. It always amused her how people would sacrifice so much if you promised to smooth that ragged pathway between nothing and something. Kef would have to check on him soon. Make sure he hadn't bragged about being recruited into Exoran's team or something equally idiotic.

The boats grew larger and the jetties and walkways grew straighter as Kef neared the Factory. She stepped onto a large pontoon at the Factory's aft. Huge and heavy-looking, the ship's steel-plated backside loomed above her, dotted with eight guards high above, frowning down at Kef.

"Hello!"

She waved up at them, smiling. Never hurt to smile. Although judging by the unchanged stoniness of their expressions, it hadn't moved them much, either.

"I'm here for a meeting with Harold Clumpwise, the alchemist!" said Kef.

"We're closed to tourists," said a guard.

Kef tilted her head to the side. Tourist, eh? She was wearing another one of her stolen outfits. This time, she had decided on a pair of practical trousers and a heavy fur jacket. Hairpins clasped her hair into a bun. On top of it all, she had the kind of feathered hat merchants wore when they were trying to show off, but thought they were being subtle with the bragging. A golden bangle wrapped around her wrist. She'd nicked that from some rich lady's wrist on the way here. She'd wanted to look local, but also authoritative; important, but also inconspicuous. Tourist was certainly not the look she was going for.

"I'm not a tourist," Kef said. "I'd like to meet with Harold, and I'm sure he'd like to meet with me."

"Too bad. We're closed indefinitely, on orders of High Captain Exoran."

"Very wise. There's been far too much scum about this city lately, if you ask me! But I really do need to see Harold. Perhaps you could tell him I'm here, and he could come to the deck where you're standing, and we could talk from there?"

She opened her jacket, exposing a sizeable purse peeking from the inner pocket. "I know Alchemy is not a cheap art, and the dealings I have with Harold would be ... appropriate, for such a fine organisation."

Some younger guards looked eagerly at the golden coins.

The main guard's expression stayed resolute. Probably could've slammed an anchor into that face and it wouldn't change.

"What's your name?" he asked.

"Katherine Hawk."

"Wait here. I'll go talk to the Head Alchemist."

The guard strode away. Kef glanced around. There was not so much as a chair on the bobbing pontoon she stood on. Typical. She squinted up at the guards. Their rifles were still trained on her, sun glinting off the barrels.

Bootsteps clattered on the ship above. Kef turned to glance up as the senior guard returned, bringing with him a woman whose shining blond hair curled into elaborate curls, tucked under a pink bowler hat that matched her pink jacket.

"Madam Hawk!" she said in a perky voice. "My name is Cordelia Le Fevre, and I'm the chief supervisor of this Factory. I apologise for the delay – these security measures are quite bothersome. Harold is inside the workshop, but I have informed him of your arrival, and he should be finished with his work soon. Please, come inside and let me entertain you until he is ready."

Kef doubted she'd find much entertainment inside an Alchemical Factory, but any offer that got her inside was worth taking. "Thank you, Madam Le Fevre."

Gears and machinery whirred from inside the ship. With a clinking of chains and rachets and cogs, a heavy steel door tilted out, rotating down until it landed onto the pontoon with a clank that wobbled the ground under Kef's feet.

The lowered door revealed a dark, square tunnel, leading into the depths of the ship. Kef's hands clutched into fists. The tunnel would present a perfect ambush opportunity. Heck,

99

they wouldn't even need to send anyone in to kill her – they could just lock her in and vent the place with poisoned gas.

Despite her reservations, Kef strode into the tunnel. As she entered, grinding gears whirred behind her. She glanced over her shoulder as the gate winched back up, plunging her into darkness.

Lights flickered on, casting a blue glow over the corridor. A slot opened beside Kef.

"Place any weapons you are carrying through the slot," said a man. "You will have them returned when leaving."

Kef put her knife through the slot. At the corridor's far end, another door opened. Kef walked through into a drab room occupied by two guards. They searched her, finding no weapons. With a grunt, they opened another door and led her up a narrow stairwell and through a maze of corridors, emerging into a plush sitting area filled with tasteful couches. Mounted on the wood-panelled walls, paintings showed scenes of storms and sunsets, old sailing yachts, and creatures of the deep reaching up with their tentacles to drag boats down beneath the waters.

Most striking of all was a painting of the sky, with scraps of ancient metals and devices falling from the Debris Belt that surrounded the planet, lighting the atmosphere with streaks of red fire as they burned on entry. That's what happened to most of the scrap that fell from the Belt to land on Entoris. But not all. Some things survived long enough to crash into the Twisted Seas, sizzling the water and drawing the attention of monsters. Kef knew because she'd done dozens of scavenging ops to reclaim skyfalls. Most of it was plain metal that was turned into boats within a few months. Half the boats in the Twisted Seas were built from fallen Belt steel; the rest came from ore mined beneath the seabed.

Skyfall hunting was a competitive, brutal game. Finding regular metals paid well enough, but finding something rare – like a handful of Ruskar Steel – could make a sailor rich enough to live the rest of her life in luxury.

And then there were relics of the Star Sailors themselves. Kef had never heard of anyone finding a working device, but some people paid ludicrous amounts for broken remnants of the machines the Sailors used to voyage between the stars – before their ships had broken into a million pieces, doomed to orbit Entoris forever.

Kef wrested her attention back to the room. Opposite from the paintings, a large glass window ran from floor to ceiling, overlooking the Factory. The gigantic room stretched to fill the ship's full width and probably two-thirds of its length; a cavern with ribs of steel running across the ceiling and walls.

Pipes snaked through the Factory, twisting and turning in chaotic shapes. Crane arms slid across overhead beams. Steam and smoke puffed into the air from vents in the pipes. Hundreds of alchemists milled about the floor, tending to machines and surveying readouts. It all looked like chaos to Kef, but it was the kind of chaos that seemed to have a secret order behind all the randomness. Just not one she could fathom.

What surprised her most was the quiet. All those moving machines and shouting people should've produced a din, but there was barely a whisper. Kef tapped the glass window. Some good soundproofing, that was.

"Quite impressive, isn't it?" said a cheery voice.

Kef turned. Cordelia waltzed into the room, hanging her pink coat on a hook by the door. She smiled. Her eyes were fractured into triangular patches of jewelled light, rotating and morphing like a kaleidoscope. Kef found the alchemical effect strangely hypnotic.

The woman gestured at the plush couches, beaming. "Please, be seated. I sent a messenger, so Harold will be along soon."

Kef glanced back out through the huge glass window. "Where is he?"

"Oh, he's not in the main area. He's doing experiments in Laboratory Gamma-Six. You know how he is! Please, sit down. A friend of Harold is a friend of mine."

Pulling her gaze away from the window, Kef sat opposite Cordelia. A servant scurried in, depositing a tray holding a half-dozen teacups on the low coffee table between their couches. Golden liquid filled the cups. Must've been some alchemical liquid, because when Kef looked into the cup, it was like she was looking down a deep well that was longer than the cup had any right to be. Arranged neatly beside the tea, glazed biscuits gleamed in the glow of the warm wall-mounted lights. When Cordelia picked one up, it changed colour to match her pink nail polish. Trust alchemists to make tea and biscuits look like some mind-bending work of art.

"Don't have anything stronger than tea, do you?" asked Kef.

"We have coffee, if you would prefer?"

"Never mind. Not the sort of strength I'm after."

The servant scurried out of the room. Kef raised a cup of tea to her lips, while Cordelia did the same.

"So, how do you know Harold?" Cordelia asked, lowering her empty cup onto the coffee table between her and Kef.

Kef stifled a groan. Was she going to suffer through half an hour of small talk? If she'd known it would be that difficult, Kef would've broken into the Factory instead.

102

"We met during a class, when I was a kid," Kef lied. "He was my sign language teacher."

Cordelia's head tilted to the side. "I didn't know he taught sign language, although I'm not surprised. From the day he became an alchemist, he has always been such a passionate teacher."

Kef raised an eyebrow. "You were around when he started working here?"

Cordelia laughed. "I appreciate the compliment, but I'm not as young as I look. Simply a beneficiary of the latest alchemical procedures."

"Could do with some of that myself."

"Don't sell yourself short, dear." Cordelia gave her a fawning smile. "You're not doing too bad, either."

Kef knew that was true. But she also knew Cordelia would praise her looks even if Kef was a three-hundred-pound slug dredged up from the sea.

Cordelia placed another empty teacup onto the table. She'd drunk two cups already. Must spend half her days pissing, with all that tea. Kef never understood tea-drinkers. Booze or water – anything between was a waste of time.

"Don't remember it being this big before," said Kef, pointing to the Factory.

"So you have visited us previously?"

"A long time ago."

Cordelia's smile deepened. "We've grown twofold since I became Chief Manager last year. It's been such a wonderful process to oversee."

The woman set to talking about alchemy and factories and recruitment. Truthfully, Kef would rather have been left alone. There'd been little time to rest over these last few days, and

103

the late nights and early mornings were getting to her. Still, a person in her position would have politely listened, so she did her best to look like she was paying attention.

"… and it should only be a few months until our serum allows for genetic interbreeding between sharks and squid!"

"Sounds impressive." Kef supressed a yawn, glancing at the clock on the wall. "Look, I don't mean to be rude, but I've got an urgent thing after this. When's Harold going to be ready?"

She'd expected some disappointment from Cordelia, but her smile remained undimmed. A servant scurried into the room, then whispered something in Cordelia's ear. She licked her lips. With a nod, she ushered the man away. The door closed with a heavy click behind him.

"What exactly were you wanting to talk to him about?" asked Cordelia. "It seems he still has some important experiments to finish up, so he will be a little longer – but we have many other alchemists, all equally as talented. Perhaps they can help?"

"I want to hire Harold for a job. Harold, specifically. I feel a debt to him, I suppose you could say, and it wouldn't feel right ignoring him over another alchemist, no matter how skilled."

"What kind of job?"

"With respect, I thought that details were kept confidential around here."

Cordelia rapped the coffee table with her knuckles. "Very true. Forgive me for prying. If I can ask just one question, however, will you be offering more than seven thousand luras?"

"No. My budget's way south of that."

Cordelia stood, her ever-present grin widening. She grabbed the bell resting on the tea tray, then rang it with a dainty flick. Footsteps squeaked in the corridor outside.

The door burst open and Kef whirled around to see the hallway filled with guards.

"That *is* a relief," said Cordelia. "Because that's well below your bounty!"

Chapter 12: ... And Reactions

Guards flooded into the room, swinging pistols up to aim at Kef. Cordelia stood and moved towards them, but before she could get out between the coffee table and her chair, Kef kicked the table, sending it crunching into Cordelia's shins. She folded over, gasping, staggering into reaching distance. Kef leaped up.

She grabbed Cordelia, wrapped one arm around her neck, and spread the other palm over the alchemist's face. "Don't move or I'll snap her neck!"

The guards froze, guns still pointing at Kef. She backed away, dragging the struggling woman with her, until she bumped up against the glass window overlooking the Factory. Cordelia's perfume swam up her nostrils, making Kef's nose wrinkle.

"Drop your guns!" Kef tightened her grip, making Cordelia squeal. "Go on, tell them to do it!"

"D-do it!" said Cordelia.

"Keep them raised, gentlemen," said someone from the corridor.

A man strode into the room. It was Henderson – Chief Warden of Blackrake Prison. A bruise around his left eye darkened his scowling expression.

"Warden Henderson." Kef forced a smile. "Give my thanks

to whoever improved your face."

Henderson glowered. "There's no thanking him. Not unless you can speak to the dead."

"My messages only go one way in that instance, I'm afraid. Speaking of which – tell these guards to put down their guns, or I'll have to make a mess of Cordelia's pretty hair."

Cordelia struggled, trying to pry Kef's arm off her throat. With her skin pressed against Kef, Kef could feel the frantic pumping of her heartbeat.

"We both know that's a false threat," said Henderson. "She's your only leverage."

Kef's mind raced. Henderson was clearly working up a plan to get the guards to shoot Cordelia and Kef. Not like he cared about the Alchemist. Most of the guards did, though, judging by their frowns and trembling hands. Best to act now, then, and act fast.

She twisted, driving up with the full force of her legs, smashing her elbow into the window behind her with a loud crunch. Cracks splintered outwards from her blow, but the glass held.

"Get her!" said Henderson.

As the guards rushed in, Kef hurled herself at the glass, holding Cordelia before her. The woman's body smashed into the window –

And the glass broke.

They fell, Kef screwing her face up tight, glass raining down around them, slicing Kef's skin, Cordelia shrieking as they plummeted. Machinery roared and workers gaped as Kef and Cordelia fell towards the floor. They crashed onto a pipe, Cordelia's body folding around the metal to soften the blow for Kef, and then they both toppled onto the floor.

107

Kef stood, groaning. Even with Cordelia to take the blow, her ribs felt battered. Not broken, but close. She grabbed onto a vent and pulled herself up, gasping, stumbling a little when her blood-slicked hand slipped off the metal. Her blood, or Cordelia's?

High above, guards raced to the edge of the observation room, pointing their guns through the broken glass. Kef scrambled behind a vat that simmered with heat, dragging Cordelia's limp body along with her.

"Don't shoot!" shouted Henderson. "We're in an Alchemical Factory! Hitting those pipes could blow this whole place up. Get down there and get the girl!"

Kef glanced around the vat. Guards sprinted out of view – clearly too scared to repeat her stunt – but Henderson stayed up there, scowling down at Kef.

"No one's ever escaped Blackrake!" he said. "And you won't, either!"

Kef gave him the finger. Then she retreated back around the vat, massaging her ribs. She kicked Cordelia.

The woman whimpered. "Don't kill me!"

"Answer this question, and I won't," said Kef. "Where's Harold?"

"I – I said! Laboratory G-g-gamma-Six, up towards the prow, level two." Tears streaked down Cordelia's face, rolling over grimacing lips. "P-please, my leg –"

Kef prodded it. Cordelia screamed.

"Yep. Definitely broken."

She slammed Cordelia's head against the vat. Kef dropped the unconscious woman, then stumbled away, winding along a narrow walkway with pipes and valves clustered on either side. In the distance, guards shouted. A klaxon wailed and emergency lighting sent a red glow washing over the Factory. Adrenaline surged through Kef.

She crawled under a pipe, down into a covered walkway beneath. From the observation room, she'd done a decent job memorising the layout, but it was a different matter navigating through the maze from down here.

Still under the pipe, she rounded the corner. A scrawny technician crouched beside a vat, peering through a glass porthole into the steaming liquid inside. He glanced at Kef. His face paled. She tackled him to the ground, pinning him underneath her and pressing her hand across his mouth.

"When I take my hand off, you're going to tell me where Laboratory Gamma-Six is. Blink if you understand."

The man blinked, staring wide-eyed up at Kef. She peeled her hand off his mouth.

"Help!" he screamed. "Somebody, h–"

Kef slammed her hand back over his mouth to muffle his cries, then shoved him against the vat. Skin sizzled, emitting the rancid smell of burning flesh. He struggled and tried to bite Kef's hand, but she was far stronger than him. She dragged him away from the vat. Tears streaked down his face.

"Do that again and I'll cook you all the way through." Kef bared her teeth at him. "Where is Laboratory Gamma-Six?"

She lifted her hand. Between whimpering gasps, the man gave her directions.

"See?" Kef pressed her hand down on his throat, choking him. "It wasn't that hard."

His hands slapped against her, but his movements were weak. Once she'd dropped him into a blackout, she sprinted away, bent double as she navigated under the pipes and the valves, the vents and the whirring fan-blades. Despite her pounding heartbeat, she grinned. It was good to show these arrogant alchemists what real power looked like.

Bootsteps clanked above her. Shouts echoed through the ship as guards raced around, trying to find Kef. Henderson roared as he directed his men.

Somehow, she reached the Factory's far end, still hiding on the lower-level walkway that led under the pipes. Kef peered through a gap, her eyes level with the floor. She'd been hoping to sneak all the way out of the Factory, but the machinery ended fifteen feet from the exit door. Three guards stood there, pistols, batons, and knives at the ready. Kef chewed her lip. If she didn't get out soon, the others would find her. What if Cordelia and the other technician had woken up? If they spilled Kef's plan, she'd have no way of reaching Harold in time.

Kef crawled back to a yellow-painted wheel she'd seen earlier. Next to it were scrawled two words: *STEAM RELEASE.*

Kef twisted the wheel. Next to her head, a pipe trembled and a hiss filled the air. Beside the door, the three guards tensed, raising their batons. The air between them and Kef grew foggy as steam poured from the vent above, though she doubted it would do much to keep her hidden. She twisted another release valve to cloud the air with more steam. The guards became faint outlines in the mist. No, the steam wouldn't hide her, but it would turn her into a murky silhouette, just like the guards. Hopefully, they'd think she was one of them.

Kef crawled out from under the pipes, emerging onto the floor. Her heart pounded. Pressed low to the ground and with the pipe behind her, she'd be hidden for now, but as soon as she stood, the guards would see her.

"Get over there!" shouted Henderson in the distance. "See

what's happening with that steam!"

Boots thumped along metal as guards raced towards her. Kef growled. Gritting her teeth, she stood and charged towards the open door. The steam cloud parted, revealing three surprised guards.

One swung his baton. Rather than dodging, Kef grabbed it and twisted into him. She striked up with her elbow, crunching into his chin, sending his optics flying off his nose, and knocking him out cold. Kef plucked the baton from his limp grip.

The next guard's baton darted towards her. She blocked that with her own, then ducked down, pulling a knife from the belt of the unconscious man. When the third guard slammed his baton into her hip, flattening her against the ground, she stabbed the knife into his boot. The blade skewered through the leather to pin his foot to the floor. He screamed, collapsing onto the ground.

Kef scrambled up. The second guard attacked again, this time with a knife. Henderson must've said to take her alive, or this guard would've led with the knife before. Now, it seemed he didn't care about following orders. Now he just cared about staying alive. Smart man.

Kef parried his blow with her baton. The blade bit into the stick, holding fast. Kef twisted the baton, wrenching the knife from his hand. She yanked the knife out of the stick, then lunged up, slicing across his chest to splatter blood onto the ground. A kick sent the man stumbling back, swallowed by the steam cloud.

Hands scrabbled at Kef's legs. She glanced down at the man whose foot she'd skewered to the floor, whose weak fingers were trying to drag her down. A kick to his head stopped that.

111

She stole his gun, and the gun from the other guard, strapping the holsters to her belt, along with their knives. Felt good to have that familiar weight at her hip.

Figures appeared nearby, cloaked by steam but growing clearer with each instant. Kef dashed into the corridor before they got any closer.

She sprinted up a stairwell, klaxon wails fading behind her. Frantic shouts bounced off the walls and she knew there wasn't long until they trapped her. She had one last trick that could help her escape, but she didn't dare use it. That would ruin everything. No, her only chance was to find Harold.

Skidding around the corner, she came to a corridor with heavy doors lining one side, each with porthole windows set into them. She could barely hear the klaxon now. Kef ran past doors, reading the signs, glancing through the portholes into the rooms as she passed. They contained small laboratories, filled with strange experiments. In one, a shark hung from chains, convulsing as electricity zapped through rods piercing its belly. In another, smoke filled the room, but as she watched, it seemed to solidify into the shape of a man. The next housed a cage containing a creature that mixed the body of a dolphin with the tentacles of an octopus.

She reached the fourth lab, sliding to a stop. Glancing at the sign to make sure, she tried the handle. Locked. Inside, a solitary man stooped over a rack of vials simmering with liquids. Earmuffs clamped over his bald head. That was Harold, alright, although he looked shorter and pudgier than she remembered. Must be approaching his late forties by now.

Kef pulled the hairpins out from her bun, pushing her hair back behind her ears before leaning close and using the pins to pick the lock. As an alchemist stumbled out of the nearest laboratory to stare at her, she slipped into the room. Kef locked the door, then dragged over a chair and slid it under the handle. Made deaf by his earmuffs, Harold stayed hunched over his vials with his back to her, using a pipette to drip red liquid into a beaker.

Kef surveyed the room. Shelves crowded the space, stacked with lead-lined boxes, ropes, and canisters bearing warning signs. Clear glass containers held dark liquids with pickled fish-corpses inside. No other exits, apart from the door she'd entered through. There was a porthole on the far wall that looked out over Zorith, but it was too small for anyone to crawl through. Kef frowned. Escape would be tricky.

On the wall hung a crayon drawing of a stick-figure man with Harold's beard, standing next to a woman with yellow hair, and a little boy. The piece was drawn in the style of a toddler with more enthusiasm than skill. Next to the door, a small potted plant sat on a table. Its blue leaves pulsed with light. An old card rested behind the plant, open to show the inside: *Thank you, Professor!* Dozens of messages filled the card.

Kef circled around the bench until she came into Harold's sight. He glanced up. A warm grin creased his smile-wrinkles and his mouth opened in pleasant surprise. He looked back down to his pipette, forehead scrunching up in concentration.

"One moment," he said in a loud voice. "Just let me balance this."

He let three drops fall into his beaker. Nothing seemed to happen, but he must have been satisfied, because he poured the beaker's contents into a canister on the bench, then sealed it with a cork.

Harold straightened up. "Kef!"

He walked around the worktable, which was bolted to the ground. She stuck out her hand, but Harold hugged her instead. After a moment of startled confusion, she hugged him back, closing her eyes and soaking up his warmth. His earmuffs rubbed against her chin, but she didn't care. She hadn't seen Harold for years.

He went to take off his earmuffs, then paused. Instead of removing them, he raised his hands, then gestured; fingers closing, then unfolding to twirl around.

"Do I still remember?" she said.

She made her hand into a fist, holding it at shoulder height, then bobbed it back and forth. *Yes.*

Earlier, Kef had told Cordelia that she met Harold in a sign language class. That was a complete lie, apart from one aspect. Harold did indeed know sign language, on account of it being a useful way to communicate in the noisy Alchemical Factory. And Kef knew it too, although for different reasons.

Harold removed his earmuffs. "I knew you would remember. Ah, Kef. It's so good to see you! To what do I owe the pleasure?"

His voice was warm and jovial, just like she remembered. Kef relaxed. She told him what she planned to do in Zorith.

Harold winced. "Are you … certain?"

"Yes."

"Why now?"

"Thought I could live without doing it. But I can't."

His eyes slid to the side. Kef glanced over her shoulder and saw a small red light flicking on and off in the corner, signalling an emergency. Harold pointed at the light, then at Kef.

"I just wanted to see you," Kef said. "I didn't want to cause any trouble, but people had other plans."

Harold glanced at the vials that surrounded him. Kef knew what he was thinking. A lifetime of experiments, and now she was here to wrest him away. His gaze flicked to the crayon drawing of his family, and the carefully cultivated plant, and the card.

Faces appeared behind the door's porthole. Guards. They pounded the glass, yelling at Kef to let them in. The thick sound-dampening door muted their cries, but they still put Kef on edge. She didn't have much time.

"Harold, you promised," she said in a shaky voice. "You said if I ever changed my mind, you'd help."

She looked down at the ground, dragging her fingers over her eyes. Must've been sweat. Not tears, because this was supposed to be a mission like any other, not something to care about enough to let herself get broken again.

Harold's hands closed around hers. She'd always thought he had strange hands for an alchemist – big and mitten-like, more suited to a blacksmith than a tinkerer, but still precise, still steady. His other finger pressed underneath her chin, tilting her head up to see his eyes.

"Not *if*. When. I always knew it would be when."

Warmth spread through Kef. For a moment she was fourteen again, alone and afraid, cold and friendless in the rain, huddled on a battered rowboat, staring up at a stranger, terrified he'd shout, terrified he'd give her to the hunters. Gritting her teeth, she forced the memory away. No room for emotions, not until this mission was over.

Behind Harold, the slamming at the door grew louder. One of the guards pounded the butt of his rifle against the porthole, fracturing the glass. It held. For now.

"You must pretend to take me against my will," Harold

115

whispered. "I have to return here in the future, to my experiments, and my family cannot be harmed."

She nodded, forcing herself to refocus. Because of the sound-dampening door, the guards couldn't have overheard Kef and Harold's quiet conversation. Time to take advantage of that.

Kef unsheathed her knife, waving it over Harold's head so the guards could see. They froze, rifles poised to smash the glass.

"Touch that glass again and he's a dead man!" she said, brandishing the knife. "Get away from the door!"

She wasn't sure if they could hear her, but they got the message. The guards lowered their rifles, backing away, still staring through the porthole. Kef's heart pounded. Not long to do this. One of them was probably trying to find the keys already.

Kef pointed her knife at Harold. In the corridor outside, someone screamed for help.

"Get your damn chemicals!" she said. "Burn a hole in that wall!"

She pointed at the wall with the porthole. That was the outer hull – barely noticeable, since at this height it had hardly any curve.

Harold gaped at Kef. "What?"

"Do it, you bastard! I know what you've got in here. I don't care how you do it, just melt a hole in that wall!"

"Okay, okay!"

Kef grabbed a coil of rope from the shelves. Harold stumbled around the lab, packing chemical kits into a bag, collecting canisters and tubes. In the corridor, one of the guards dashed away. Probably to warn the others so they could get someone to the hull outside. Kef licked her lips. They had to escape

116

before that happened.

Slinging his bag over his shoulder, Harold tipped liquids into canisters, adding sprinkles of powder and herbs. His large hands moved with surprising deftness. Kef watched, eyes narrowed, as he tucked a beaker filled with oil underneath the bench. Next, he stoppered a tube filled with viscous yellow liquid, then clamped it upside-down above the beaker.

Kef licked her lips again. She had a lot of respect for Harold's calmness. Dealing with these chemicals looked easy, but if you screwed up there wouldn't be much warning before the explosion ripped you apart.

The door clicked. Kef glanced up, cursing when she saw the handle trying to turn. Someone was attempting to open it with a key, ducking down so Kef couldn't see them through the porthole. Would've worked, too, if it wasn't for the handle being jammed against the back of a chair, preventing it from turning.

Kef raised her gun. "I've got a pistol! Drop the key or I'll shoot the whole damn lot of you!"

Curses sounded from the corridor. The handle stopped straining against the chair.

Harold crossed to the outer wall, holding two beakers sloshing with dark liquids. He poured them together, then splashed the result onto the metal wall. Nothing happened. Kef chewed her lip. Had he got it wrong? What if his skill didn't match her memory? Or worse – what if he didn't want to follow Kef's plan at all, and this had merely been a charade to buy time?

A hissing noise came from the wall. Kef exhaled a relieved breath as the acid ate into the metal, gnawing through the hull The steel melted to form a hole, providing a view of the boats crowded on the water. With each second the hole widened. When it was big enough for both of them to crawl through, Harold tossed another mixture onto the metal to nullify the acid. Steam billowed up from the six-inch-thick steel. When it died away, the hissing stopped. Kef tapped her knife against the wall, right where the acid had stained it black. Her knife stayed intact.

Kef lashed the rope to Harold's worktable, which was bolted to the ground. She tossed the rope through the new opening. It spiralled through the air, crashing against the roof of a boat far below. Good thing the Factory was surrounded by hundreds of vessels all pressed up against its hull. Disappearing within that chaotic mess would be easy. But they'd need a distraction to draw everyone's attention away – otherwise, the guards on the deck above would see where Kef and Harold were going.

Harold ducked beneath his workbench. From the upside-down tube fixed above the beaker, he pulled out the stopper. The liquid stayed suspended in the tube, too thick to fall.

"Five drops," he whispered.

The base of the sticky yellow liquid stretched down, moving with the slowness of tar, and then a single drop plinked into the beaker, mixing with the oil.

Kef aimed her knife at Harold, baring her teeth. "Get down that rope, now!"

Raising his arms, Harold shuffled over to the rope. He grabbed onto it, then scurried outside. Kef hoped he was fit enough for the descent. It wasn't far, but Harold didn't look in the best of shape. More bootsteps pounded in the corridor outside and a cautious head appeared in the porthole, right as a second drop fell into the beaker.

The guard's eyes widened. "Harold's not there! It's just the girl!"

"Then rush her!" said Henderson's voice.

Another drop plinked into the beaker.

Something slammed into the door, knocking the chair away from under the handle. Kef glanced through the opening in the wall. Harold had almost reached the boat below.

A key clicked in the lock. The handle rotated.

"The chair's gone!" said a guard. "Open it!"

The fourth drop fell into the beaker as the entrance door squeaked open. Guns stuck through the gap. Kef raised her own pistol and fired at the door, making the hands withdraw.

"Shoot her!" yelled Henderson.

The fifth drop formed on the tip of the tube. Guns poked back around the door. Hoping she'd placed her trust in the right person, Kef turned, then dove through the hole in the wall, wrapping her hands around the rope. She swung around, slamming against the hull, then plummeted. Rope burned her hands.

In the room above, there was a huge crash as the guards kicked open the door. As she slid down the rope, boots banging against the hull, Kef glanced up. A guard's head emerged through the hole. He swung his gun down to point at her.

A thunderous explosion shook the air.

Black smoke burst from the hole, obscuring the man, erupting to darken the air around Kef. Guards screamed. The gas erupted out from the lab, filling the air with a fog so thick the rope was a murky outline before Kef. Wouldn't be fatal, but Harold's chemicals had worked. She didn't know how he had formulated it to explode after exactly the fifth drop, but there was a reason why he was an alchemist and she was a thief.

Her boots slammed into a metal roof, sending her sprawling. Hands dug under her sweaty armpits to haul her up. Harold's pudgy face was scarcely a shadow in the gloomy blackness. Too dark to tell, but there was a worried crease above his eyes. He glanced up at the Factory, which was obscured by the cloud.

Kef tapped his shoulder, bringing his eyes back to hers. "You good?"

He nodded. Kef doubted that was the case. Hopefully, the alchemists would think this was a kidnapping, so that after her mission Harold could return to his work. And – more importantly – his family. She grabbed his hand, then led him off the roof, away from the sirens, away from Henderson's distant roaring, and away from the Factory.

Chapter 13: Strange Gifts

Kef barged into Gabine's room. "Grab your things. We're leaving."

Gabine looked up from her desk. Spread before her were plans and drawings, cataloguing the Lightning Tower from every angle and detail.

"What's wrong?"

"The Blackrake wardens have followed us here. We need a more secure location."

Gabine's gaze shifted over Kef's shoulder, to where Harold stood in the corridor, wearing a broad-brimmed hat and a baggy tunic to hide his alchemical lab coat.

"Another helper," said Kef.

Gabine rolled up her plans, placing them into a long tube. "You're gathering helpers like a dog collects fleas."

"This is the last one. Now, less snark and more packing."

Kef strode through the corridor to Squine's room. Harold paced beside her.

"She seems grumpy," he said.

"Shouldn't be. I rescued her from prison."

Harold raised his eyebrows. "Some would say she got the worse end of that deal."

Kef snorted. "I knew I should've taken a different alchemist."

121

Squine's door was locked. Kef pounded on it.

"Get your things, kid. We're moving."

No response. Kef knocked again, gritting her teeth. She'd got herself and Harold here in record time, but they couldn't delay. Above Zorith, the air was thick with wingers soaring over the city, searching for her, and the patrolling guards on the ground had doubled in numbers. They'd probably be plastering wanted posters up on walls within the hour.

Still nothing from inside the room. Kef picked the lock, then stormed inside. Squine floated on his back in the room's freestanding bath, ears underwater, gazing vacantly up at the ceiling. Calling it a bath was probably too generous. More like a stagnant pond the innkeeper cleaned once a decade. Still, the kid looked annoyingly peaceful. Kef grabbed the front of his swimsuit and hauled him up out of the filthy water.

"We're leaving!" she said. "Get your things."

Harold's lips pressed together. Kef knew he didn't like how Zorith treated gillers. She could hardly complain about that, given how his sympathies for the downtrodden had benefitted her hugely. Still, she hoped he wasn't going to make a big deal about it.

He extended his hand. "I'm Harold Clumpwise."

Squine shook his hand tentatively. Weren't many people who offered their hands to gillers. Mostly it had to do with their constant clamminess, although a few fools thought being a giller was contagious.

Harold made a strange, garbled noise from the back of his throat.

Squine's yellow eyes widened. "You know the Flowing?"

"Only a handful of phrases, I'm afraid."

Kef snapped her fingers at Squine, then pointed to the clock hanging on the wall. "Downstairs. Three minutes."

Kef strode down to the inn's main room. An old drunk hunched in the corner, next to a stack of empty bottles. Behind the bar, the innkeeper scrubbed the wood, trying to remove a stain. He wasn't having much luck.

The innkeeper looked up. "Is something wrong? I heard shouting."

Kef grunted. "You could say that. Can we talk privately?"

The innkeeper beckoned Kef behind the bar, then opened a trapdoor. She followed him down the ladder. She'd expected a storage room, but it looked like another guest room, although much more spacious. His own home, perhaps? A quick glance around confirmed that suspicion – there were too many strange knick-knacks for this to be rented to guests.

"What can I help you with?" he asked.

Kef turned so he wouldn't see her slip the knife out of her sleeve.

"Something urgent came up. I know we paid for a week, but we need to leave now."

"Ah, I see."

Judging by his frown, he could tell that wasn't the full truth. You didn't ask for confidentiality to organise room bookings.

"You want a refund?" he asked.

Kef let the knife slip out a further, until the grip rested in her hand. She took no relish in this. But that was how things had to unfold. If guards came knocking, or the innkeeper discovered the bounty on Kef's head, he'd ruin everything. Kef didn't have much over the wardens hunting for her, but as far as she knew, they didn't realise she'd freed Gabine. If they figured that out, and told Exoran, he'd connect the dots and the Lightning Tower would become twice as hard to sneak into. Twice as hard, when it was already near impossible. After all the pain Exoran had inflicted, if she couldn't get into the Tower and wrest away Zorith's power, she'd never be able to live with herself.

"Yes," said Kef. "A refund, please."

The man opened his purse and counted out the luras. Kef sighed. Part of her wanted him to take longer, as if letting the man steal a couple more breaths would make her deed less dark. The other part of her laughed at that notion. She'd done a lot worse for a lot less. Besides, killing this man to keep him silent was equally dark, whether she did it now or in a few moments.

Kef scowled. It all came back to Exoran, to the Lightning Tower, to Zorith. They'd turned her into this. They'd made her plunge her hands into the world's filth. And they got to sit in their luxury ships, and stare down at the slums and shanty-boats, ignoring the brutality that kept them wealthy and heedless. Kef took a deep breath. Stealing the Channeler from the Lightning Tower would change that. But like all change, first there was sacrifice.

"Here you go."

The innkeeper gave Kef a handful of luras. He cocked his head to the side, and she realised her breath was coming loud and quick.

"Thanks." Kef paused. "I'm sorry, but there's one more thing –"

Behind the innkeeper, the door opened. A small girl walked out, dressed in a one-piece costume coloured hideously pink. She stared wide-eyed at Kef, then at the innkeeper.

"Who's that, Daddy?"

"That's Kirsty. She's one of my guests. Say hello to her."

124

The little girl stared down at her slippers. "Hello to her."

The innkeeper laughed.

A sour taste filled Kef's mouth. "This is your daughter?"

"Sometimes the fates bless us, don't they?"

He hoisted the girl up onto his hip, smiling broadly.

Kef chewed her lips. "Sometimes they do."

The girl's eyes darted down. Her eyes widened. She glanced up at Kef, and Kef knew she'd seen the knife she was holding by her side. Kef's face twitched. Should've held it closer. Not that it would've made much difference. Had to do this, and there was no way around it.

The girl's scared eyes bored into Kef. How old was she? Six? Seven, maybe? With those wide eyes, the way she clutched at her father's shirt, like it would shield her from all the perils of the world … It was easy to see a different girl in her place. A girl just as scared, just as fearful, just as attached to someone who was supposed to protect them.

Kef slipped the knife into its sheath.

She handed her change back to the man. "Keep it."

There was a burning in her throat. She swallowed, but the burning didn't go away.

"I can't take this," said the innkeeper. "It's not fair."

Kef coughed. Still didn't clear that lump in her throat. How could she have even considered killing the innkeeper? What was this mission doing to her?

She strode to the ladder, then clambered up the rungs, boots stomping on the wood.

"Don't take it for the rooms," she said. "Get a present for your daughter."

Chapter 14: A New Disguise

Always have a backup. That's what Plank had drilled into Kef. Hadn't done so well for him in the end, but it was good advice none the less.

Kef peered around the corner, checking the jetties were clear. It had been a hard, long slog, dragging her crew through this city with guards swarming everywhere, skies thick with wingers and waters clogged with gillers. But it looked like the path to their safehouse was clear enough.

She beckoned for the others to join her. Following her lead, Squine, Harold, and Gabine crept out of an alley formed between two broken-down barges, and out onto a pontoon that strained to keep hold of the three jetties sprouting from its side. They shaded their eyes against the low-angled evening sunlight.

Kef led them to a small dingy, bobbing in the water beside the jetty. She pulled back the tarpaulin covering the boat, then ushered them inside. It was a tight squeeze, especially given Harold's girth, which almost capsized the dingy when he stepped in.

"Where are we going?" asked Gabine.

Kef pointed across a stretch of open water. On the far side was a hulking cargo ship, dozens of tall silos standing high on its deck, and dozens more anchored to the side of its hull. Faded numbers were painted onto the silos. Waves slapped up against them, making dull ringing noises, and when the breeze changed direction, a rotten-egg smell wafted up Kef's nostrils.

"The seaweed silos?" asked Harold.

Kef nodded.

"I thought we were finding a place to hide," said Squine.

"We are. In one of those silos."

Gabine frowned. "I've seen their schematics. They're filled with seaweed, and even if they were empty, they're sealed with double-skinned metal."

"Fourty-six of them are. But the fourty-seventh ... well, let's just say – a few months back, it had an accident. I might've been involved. Not for this job, but another. I checked a week ago, right before I went to get you, Gabine. They haven't fixed it. Lazy gits, but I suppose it's been a turbulent time in Zorith. Besides, there wasn't any seaweed in this silo before, so I guess they don't need the room. Either way, lucky for us. One of those nice silos has a hole in the bottom, big enough for us to get through."

"I don't understand." Squine frowned. "If there's a hole, why haven't they repaired it?"

"They probably haven't seen it. It's underneath the silo, a few feet below the waterline."

"Then why hasn't it sunk?"

"The silos are all linked together," said Gabine. "And to the ship. The others are holding it up."

Kef patted her on the back. "Looks like those years of architecting hasn't gone to waste."

Gabine squinted at the silos. "Huh. You're talking about silo

127

thirty-eight, right?"

"Um, yes?"

Gabine snorted. "Mustn't be any decent engineers left in this city. I can tell that from here."

Kef glanced at the silo again. Gabine was right, but Kef didn't know how she'd seen it, because the empty silo looked identical to all the others.

"Squine, poke your head in the water and tell us if we've got a clear path," she said.

Kef leaned against the boat's starboard side so that Squine could lean over the port railing without capsizing the boat. The boy lowered his head underwater.

A few moments passed before he drew back up. "There's at least three gillers between our boat and the silos. They're wearing guard uniforms and they seem to be on patrol."

Kef chewed her lip. Expected, but still annoying. She reached underneath a bench, pulling out a waterproof satchel.

"Stay here," she said. "I'll be back in a minute."

She climbed out of the dingy, then pulled the tarp back over the boat to hide Harold, Gabine, and Squine. Slinging the satchel over her shoulder, she retraced her steps along the walkways they'd used to get here. This district was a middle-class suburb, mainly for merchants and their families, with four-story-tall houseboats fixed to orderly jetties. Several boats proudly flew Zorith's blue and white flag.

Once she'd walked a decent distance, she untied the satchel, then unsealed the plastic bag inside. A rank stench of rotting meat and putrid chemicals made her gag. She dumped it in the water. Coughing, she scrambled back through the district to return to the dingy.

"Give it a few minutes," she said, climbing inside and pulling the tarp over to hide her team.

"What did you do?" asked Harold.

"Dumped two kilos of ammonium-soaked fish guts in the water. Sharks will be swarming Zorith in seconds. Might even get some other sea monsters if we're lucky."

Squine's yellow eyes widened. "But th-they banned that!"

Kef raised her eyebrows. "Don't know if you noticed, kid, but what we're doing isn't strictly legal."

Squine shuddered, then stared down at the floor. He was probably imagining the enraged beasts shooting beneath the city, converging on the fish guts, bloodlust stirred from the chemical scent. Gillers tended to react like that when you mentioned sharks. They were up to the task of killing them, of course, especially if armed with harpoons, but for all their mutations, gillers were still strangers to the sea. For sharks, it was their domain.

A distant scream tore through the air. Whistles shrieked, people yelled, and gunshots cracked, all distorted by the wind.

Kef crossed her arms behind her head, then leaned back against the boat. "Poke your head underwater, Squine. See if those gillers have left."

Squine gulped. Was he thinking about refusing? Kef doubted he had experience with sharks. Too flimsy for that – not like those other gillers she kept wishing the Kazzia had given her.

She shifted position, letting light glint off the canister in her pocket, where she kept the Zetamyre. Squine's shoulders sagged. Taking a deep breath that rippled the gills on his neck, he pushed up the tarpaulin covering the boat, then leaned over the side.

Harold glared at Kef. "You're using Zetamyre?"

129

"Not by choice. The Kazzia keeps all her gillers addicted for security."

"It's not right."

"You know I don't like Z, but what choice do I have? I can hardly wean the kid off."

Harold shook his head. With his hands, he signed, *I did for you.*

Gabine frowned. "What? Is that sign language?"

"Private message," said Kef.

A memory of vomit, stomach cramps, and cold sweats stabbed into her mind. The first days after she'd met Harold was a blur, but one detail remained. Harold's hand on her shoulder – a patch of warmth in the biting darkness.

Weaning me off took weeks, she signed. *We don't have time.*

Squine slithered back into the boat, water dripping from his head. "They're gone."

Kef folded back the boat's tarp, then slotted oars into brackets. Harold untied the mooring ropes. Arms straining, Kef heaved at the oars. Their boat slid away from the jetty, out into the choppy water.

"Get over the side and push," she said to Squine.

"What about the sharks?"

"They're half a district away. You'll be fine, and you'll be a sight finer the sooner we reach those silos."

Squine dove overboard. The boat picked up speed as he pushed against the aft. Waves crashed into the prow, spilling cold water against Kef's neck.

"Anything you need keeping, put in those waterproof bags under the back bench," she said to Harold and Gabine. "We're going under in thirty seconds."

Gabine stashed her drawing tube in a bag, while Harold

did the same with his alchemical kit. Kef glanced over her shoulder. Halfway to the seaweed silos, and making good time.

Wingers soared overhead. Kef tensed, but they flew past, heading towards the distant screams.

She angled the dingy towards silo thirty-eight. While they had been moored on the other side of the water, she'd observed the workers patrolling along the ship. Based on the patterns she'd found, they should have a decent window to get across without the workers seeing them, and even if they were spotted, the workers would hopefully assume Kef's dinghy was just passing by.

They bumped against metal with a soft clang. Kef glanced over her shoulder to see the boat's prow grinding against silo thirty-eight. She reached into the water to tap Squine's head. Dumb kid was still pushing against the aft. His head surfaced as he looked up at Kef.

"Check under the silo," she said. "There should be a hole in the middle, wider than this boat."

The boy slipped underwater.

Kef glanced back at Harold and Gabine. "Got everything secured?"

They nodded.

Squine emerged beside the boat. "The hole's there."

"Good. Now, this next part's tricky, but just do your best to hold on tight and we'll come through it fine."

Hopefully, at least. Last time she'd done this, it'd been with a crew much younger and fitter than a seventy-two-year-old architect and a somewhat rotund alchemist. Well, too late to back down now.

Kef reached down and pulled a plug from the boat's floor.

Water spewed from the hole, bubbling into the boat.

Gabine cursed. "We're going to sink!"

"That's the idea. Can't leave the boat tethered out here or someone will find it." Kef sat upright and rolled her shoulders to ease the kinks in her muscles. "But don't panic. Well, as long as you can hold your breath for more than twenty-three seconds, don't panic."

Harold and Gabine glanced at each other.

"We can both do it," said Harold with a warm smile.

"Yes," growled Gabine. "So I don't know who you're talking to, Kef."

"Just checking," she said.

Water flooded into the boat, lapping against Kef's boots, rising up her shin, cold against her skin. The boat sank. Kef hooked her feet under a bench and Gabine and Harold did the same.

"When we get under, guide us to the hole," said Kef to Squine. "Then push us up into it."

The last thing she saw before the water rose above her eyes was Squine, yellow eyes narrowing as he nodded. She hoped the kid had enough strength to push the boat.

They sunk through the water. Air bubbled from Kef's nose. Beside their dingy, the silo was a dark mass of pitted metal, crusted with barnacles and swarms of fish that darted through little hovels formed amongst the growth. Was it Kef's imagination, or could she hear distant screams echoing through the water? She glanced over her shoulder in the direction where she'd thrown the shark bait. Didn't help much. Couldn't see more than a few paces through the water's murk. Even Gabine and Harold were reduced to blurred shadows.

Their dingy dropped below the silo's base. Squine swam

under the boat, pushing at the bottom, halting their fall. He heaved them underneath the silo. Kef took an alchemical glow cube from her pocket, then shook it. Light flared from inside the dice-sized cube, casting a pale blue glow across Harold and Gabine, and across the barnacle-encrusted base of the silo above. Squine pushed the boat through a jagged-edged hole. Seconds later, Kef's head broke the surface.

She wrinkled her nose at the stench of old seaweed. Water sloshed against metal with a hollow ping as Kef raised her glow cube, illuminating the storage silo. They were at the bottom of a tall cylinder, with the ceiling lost in darkness above. Two walkways circled around the walls, joined by a rusted ladder that led down into the water. A few sorry strands of seaweed floated around them.

Kef and the others bailed water out of the boat, while Squine kept it propped up from below. Once it could float without the giller's support, Kef lashed it to the ladder. She climbed up. Rust flaked off the metal as her boots hit the rungs.

Her supply crates were up on the walkway, just like she'd left them. Inside, there would be enough canned food to last for the next few days. And – more importantly – a decent stash of weapons.

Kef glanced down. Gabine and Harold looked up from the dingy, which bobbed in the glistening water. Squine floated beside the boat. Kef's glow cube painted their faces in a ghostly blue light.

Harold unpeeled a chemtab – two thin sheets of plastic, stuck together with an alchemical paste – making steam rise from his hands as the chemicals reacted with the air. He gave one sheet of the chemtab to Gabine, who mumbled thanks as she gripped the hand warmer.

133

"What now, Kef?" asked Harold.

Kef climbed the ladder to the topmost walkway. There was a tiny hole in the wall where a rivet had fallen out. Through the hole, she saw a distant spire standing tall and sharp against the cloudy sky, glowing from the last rays of the evening light.

The Lightning Tower.

"First, we sleep," she said. "Then tomorrow, we plan."

Chapter 15: Schemes in the Silo

"I don't see how that last part can work," said Harold, frowning at a cross-sectional drawing of the Lightning Tower. "The Channeler is too big to extract that way."

"You've never seen it," said Kef.

"No. But Gabine said it fills this room." Harold pointed to a windowless chamber near the top of the Lightning Tower, on the floor under the glass-domed room that crowned the whole structure. "She was very specific about the size. And as you can see, the room's fifty feet wide."

Kef glanced at Gabine. "Did you see the device?"

"No. They installed it after I was exiled, the scumbags."

Kef shrugged. "Don't worry. I know what it looks like, and it'll be easy enough to move around, especially once we've breached the Tower. Any other objections?"

She'd spent the last hour defending the plan from Gabine and Harold's critiques. Squine had stayed wordless. Probably too stressed about his role in it all.

"You trust the aristocrat?" asked Harold.

"I trust his greed. And I'm planning a visit before the heist. After that, I'll trust his fear as well. Anything else?"

Their questions annoyed her. None of them knew the first thing about a heist. None of them knew how many years Kef had turned this scheme over in her mind. None of them knew why she was really doing this, either. She planned to keep it like that until the mission finished.

When no one voiced any more annoying questions, she stood, pulling on the ladder to haul her aching body up. "The city's going to be hot today while they search for Harold. We'll rest up here. When they can't find you, they'll assume I took you out of Zorith and the heat will ease. Tomorrow, we'll move into position for the heist; we'll need to set up our operations a few hours before Exoran's party in the evening. Now, grab something to eat and have a rest. Keep as quiet as possible. We don't know when the workers are going to walk overhead. I'll go on first watch."

Harold waddled around the walkway to the supply crates, where he set to work dragging spare cloaks over the metal floor to form bedding. Squine dove over the walkway's railing, slicing into the water with barely a ripple or splash. He came up a few seconds later, floating on his back, those lidded yellow eyes gazing up at the ceiling. Gabine stayed where she was, watching Kef roll up the drawings.

"This whole affair reminds me of when I was young," said Gabine. "Working in my studio, with my designers and my apprentices ... you know, whenever we took in a new apprentice, I could always tell whether they'd make it, even before I was the boss."

Kef slipped the drawings into a tube, then handed it to Gabine. "Good thing I'm not an apprentice."

"All of them came into the office saying how much they cared about design," continued Gabine, like she'd not even heard Kef. "How designing boats was all they ever wanted to do with their lives. But you could tell. You could tell which

136

ones were happy to stay late at night, sweep the workshop, and love everything else about the process. Then there were the others. The others who left on time, every day, and went out to parties while we kept working. It's funny. The more a new person liked to brag about being an architect, the worse they were. You could always tell which ones loved the process, and which ones loved the prestige."

The old woman turned over to stare at Kef. Her wrinkles were deep and dark in the faint yellow light.

"You're not in this for the money, Kef."

Kef climbed down the ladder. "Go to sleep, old woman."

"You can act all you want, but you can't fool me, and you don't need to."

Kef stepped onto the dingy to sort the supplies. She tried opening a bag, but her fingers kept slipping. Scowling, she finally dug her fingers through the knot, then ripped it open.

She glanced up. Gabine shuffled along the walkway, towards where Harold lay on his makeshift bed, chest rising and falling with gentle slowness. Kef scratched the back of her left hand, staring down at the pale, mottled skin. Keep it together. That's all she had to do for another few days and then she'd be free again.

She sighed. That's what she'd told herself fifteen years ago, the night before she escaped. And it had been true. Free to roam the seas, free to live without a master, but apparently not free of the past. This would do it, though. This would free her from the screams, the nightmares, the agony of waking with a heaving chest and clammy skin, and the fear that the last fifteen years had been a delusion.

And if it didn't free her from that, she didn't know what would.

For the Kazzia's consideration

Spurmonger

Also known as a 'rain fish,' the spurmonger shoots torrents of water into the air from its twin sprayholes. This creates an artificial rain, designed to attract small fish to the surface, which the spurmonger feasts upon. Large spurmongers have been known to sink small boats from the force of their sprayed water.

Mondoceros

The fast-swimming mondoceros uses their long horn to spear prey. As well as being a useful hunting tool, they tap their horns against the horns of other mondoceroses during their elaborate mating rituals. Their prospective mate will determine whether they are a worthy partner based on the tempo and the accuracy of their rhythm.

Yappener

Yappeners enjoy the company of humans and will often congregate in the wake of city-ships. While they are rarely able to be fully domesticated, regular feeding can make yappeners moderately loyal to some humans, to the point where they will recognise faces and perform tricks for their feeders, even years after going without contact.

Flying Fish

Small proto-wings allow this species of fish to glide through the air. While they are unable to achieve full flight, this capability allows them to evade predators and eat low-flying insects. They are rarely dangerous to humans, although a swarm of flying fish can easily get stuck on a boat's deck, leading to a great deal of chaos.

Chapter 16: Long Lost

"Kef?"

Kef paused with her sharpening stone halfway along her knife. She leaned over the side of the walkway to stare down at Squine, floating in the water below. He'd been underneath the dark surface for the last hour, probably lying on the silo's base. Overhead, gentle rain drummed against the metal roof.

"What?" she whispered.

She didn't want to wake Harold or Gabine, who were sleeping on the other side of the walkway.

"I just remembered." Squine swallowed. "Back at the inn, I think I left something there."

Kef thought of the innkeeper.

She scowled. "Too bad. Make do without it."

"I would, master, only ... it's got my name."

"What?"

"It's a locket, with my name engraved on the casing."

Kef cursed. Anything else might've been fine. But an engraved locket was clearly valuable, and that could hurt them, because the innkeeper struck her as someone who'd try to return the locket to its owner. He'd probably visit a directory to find Squine's name, where he'd discover the boy was indentured to the Kazzia. That would raise all manner of dangerous questions.

Could they risk ignoring it?

Kef checked her pocket watch. "Why did you wait until now to tell me?"

Squine's shoulders sagged. "I only remembered now, master. I'm sorry."

Kef wanted to leap down into the water and strangle the kid, but she forced herself to breathe. One, because she remembered the snap of Exoran's whip all too well. And two – it'd be a damn noisy affair.

"I think I know how to get back without running into patrols," he said. "There's a route that flows under the sewerage vents. None of us gillers like to use it, because it's disgusting – but it might let us get back quickly."

Kef stood, groaning. She scribbled a quick note for Harold and Gabine, leaving it on the walkway, then clambered onto the ladder. "If we get caught, you're so dead."

Squine forced an uneasy smile. "Won't we be dead anyway?"

"I'll find a way to kill you again."

#

With a click, the lock slid open. Kef slipped through the fire escape door. Squine shuffled in behind her. She crept through the corridor, keeping her footsteps soft against the ground.

"So what's a giller like you doing with a locket?" Kef asked. "Present from your girlfriend?"

The kid squirmed. "Yes. Well, no, but … yes. Sort of."

Kef snorted. "That's four answers to choose from."

She crouched beside a panel marked with danger signs and thunderbolts. How appropriate. Her picks made short work of it, and soon they were crawling up a maintenance ladder, using an alchemical glow-cube to illuminate the shaft with orange light.

The kid's route had worked. Somehow they'd reached the *Lucky Robust* – the ship where the *Poor Canary* was – and now all they had to do was creep through the corridors until they reached the inn. Kef was probably being paranoid, all things considered. The innkeeper didn't strike her as the kind to rat out his clients, especially when his business hadn't exactly been booming. Still, if she had to choose between optimistic and dead or anxious and alive, she'd pick the latter.

"The locket was from a girl back in Ivourium," said Squine. "That's where I grew up before … before my gills came and my parents sold me to the Asadi."

Kef glanced down. Squine had paused on the ladder, staring at his webbed hands. Hard to grip the rungs, with fingers like those. From her glow cube, orange light glinted off his scales.

"C'mon, keep moving," Kef said.

He shook, startled, then scrambled up to match Kef's pace.

"I mean, it wasn't really a present from her." Squine's voice was shaky. "I … I got it for her, right before the Asadi took me. But she gave it back."

Kef snorted. "Unlucky, kid."

"No, it's not like that! I know she likes me. It's just she couldn't … not while I'm a giller. But when I'm free, when I have money, I'll go back to Ivourium. Back to her."

Kef squinted at the number painted beside an access hatch. Level three. Still a way to go.

"She a giller, too?"

"No."

"Seems like you're sailing against the wind, then."

Squine's slimy hands slapped against the rungs with wet

squelches. Wordless silence stretched between them as they climbed.

"It hurts, sometimes." Squine's voice quivered. "Thinking about her. I know she still loves me, but sometimes I wonder if … if she's forgotten. Or if it was never real to begin with. And every day I spend out here makes it worse."

Squine swallowed, his gills fluttering with a damp sucking noise that echoed through the ladder-shaft. "Sorry, master, you probably don't want to hear this –"

"It's fine, kid. But I'll give you some advice: if love makes you hurt, you're doing it wrong. More than likely there's a thousand people out there who'll want you, and pining after someone who doesn't is a recipe for madness. Life's short. Don't waste it on people who don't care about you, because it'll be done in an eyeblink and you'll wish you enjoyed it more. Trust me, I've seen men die, and to see regret in their eyes … it's a scary thing."

She thought about Plank, those glassy eyes staring up at the sky, mouth agape, spittle dribbling down his suntanned face. All the vitality draining away until he was pale and stiff. Back to the waters with him. Just like all the others who'd left her.

Kef reached the level five access panel. She pressed her ear up against it. Sounded like a group was walking by, but after a few moments their footsteps faded away. Kef went to push on the access panel, then paused.

She glanced down at Squine. The boy stared at his hands, examining the webbing that stretched between his fingers, pale and translucent in the glow cube's light. What would it feel like, for your body to morph into something strange? Something alien? For all of Kef's struggles, at least she'd never experienced that.

Although she'd still had to endure all the other abuses that came with her differences. The whippings, the fear of being shot, the windowless room pressing tight around her, dark and blinding at the same time. Knowing that in the scheme of it all, you were less than the common person. Either everyone else didn't know about your existence, or they knew you were their slave and they still didn't care. Or worse – they relished it. Nothing quite so primal as knowing another human was beneath you.

Kef gazed at the mottled skin on the back of her hand. She thought about Exoran. About the Lightning Tower. About the scared girl she'd once been. When she looked down at Squine again, it didn't take much imagination to see the resemblance.

"Hey, Squine."

The boy looked up, his yellow eyes wide with worry. "Wh-what is it, master?"

Kef's face twitched. "Can you drop the 'master?' Just call me Kef."

"Yes, m –" The boy paused. "Yes, Kef."

Something welled up in the back of her throat. Probably a ball of phlegm, aching to be spat. Burnt like fire, though.

Kef placed her hand back on the access panel, while Squine looked up at her, wide-eyed and chewing his fingernails.

"You're a good kid, Squine." Kef didn't know why she was saying it, but she felt like she had to. "I know I'm an arsehole to you, but … you're a decent kid, alright?"

Squine gaped. Kef waited for him to respond, but then a few seconds went by with neither of them speaking, so she pushed the access panel open, stepping into an empty corridor lit by dim lights. Squine followed her, wrapping his arms around himself. Kef walked towards the *Poor Canary's* door, scowling.

Why couldn't she find the right words to cheer him up?

Squine's lack of thanks annoyed her. Then she considered it more and realised how self-centred that was, which compounded the whole issue. She sighed. Why did everything make her mad at herself?

A thought struck Kef. Maybe once this mission was done, she didn't have to return Squine to the Kazzia. Maybe she could free him from Zorith instead. Wean him off Zetamyre, the way Harold had freed Kef from her addiction, and take the kid into her proper crew. The Sea Scars already had a giller, but another wouldn't go amiss. Treel would be more than willing to welcome the kid into the team.

Warmth filled Kef. Yes. Maybe she didn't have the words or the compassion to help the boy right now, but getting him out from the Kazzia's shackles, training him as one of her crew – maybe she could help the kid grow from boy to man. Just like what Plank had done for Kef.

Her fingers curled around the inn's doorknob. Before she could open it, Squine's cold hand touched her shoulder. She glanced back at him.

"Th-thanks. For before." Squine looked down. "Sorry."

"It's alright." Kef pushed the door open. "C'mon."

There was no one behind the bar, no lights shining overhead. A big stain of spilled drink spread across the dirty floorboards, shimmering bronze in her glow cube's light. Seemed a little odd to keep the front door unlocked without anyone minding the room, but it suited Kef just fine.

She shook the glow cube to remove the light. Her eyes adjusted to the dim blueness shining through the porthole from the city-ship outside. She climbed the stairs, keeping to the edges to reduce the creaking. Couldn't stop it all, though.

Each groan of metal made her teeth clench tighter together. And then there were Squine's squelching footsteps. Maybe he was a decent kid, but he sure wasn't a quiet one. Still, everyone should be sleeping at this time of night, so hopefully they'd be too drowsy to hear them creeping up the stairs.

She strode along the corridor to Squine's room. There was no *DO NOT DISTURB* sign hanging off the handle. Hopefully, that meant no one was inside. Kef crouched, sliding her lockpick into the keyhole. A few quiet jigs worked it open.

"Alright," whispered Kef to Squine. "Do this quick, do this quiet."

Squine swallowed, then nodded. Kef stood, then pushed the door open, stifling a yawn. Should've spent the night sleeping, not creeping around Zorith.

Inside the room, a light flicked on. Six guards sat on chairs, with their guns pointed at Kef.

Chapter 17: Foolish Dreams

K ef gaped at the guards. Squine shoved her and she stumbled forward, sprawling into the middle of the room. She glanced back as Squine slammed the door shut, his scaly face pale with fear.

"You slimy little fucker!" she yelled.

The guards scrambled up from their seats, clicking the safety off their guns as they pointed them down at Kef. Staying on all fours, Kef's eyes swivelled to either side, fixing the room's layout in her mind. Crammed and stinking of seaweed, the freestanding bath filled with scummy water was still tucked in one corner. In the opposite corner, the bed was unmade. Why hadn't the innkeeper fixed that? Had these guards killed him already?

Illuminating the whole scene, a single lightbulb stuck out from the flimsy plaster-panelled ceiling. A tiny porthole punched through the wall, too small to climb through. Six guards stood around Kef. Squine was outside the room, probably watching through the keyhole.

"Told you the giller would deliver, didn't I?" said a guard with a thick beard.

"Pay up, Reedy!" said another guard in a squealing voice. "Pay up, pay up!"

"Shut up, Max," said Reedy. "You got lucky! Everyone thought this lead was bust, or he would've sent more of us. Tony – cuff her."

Tony's boots squeaked across the floor. Kef didn't dare raise off the ground any higher than her elbows. The room was crammed, but not so crammed that any of them were within striking distance. Especially with six guns pointed at her.

Handcuffs clinked as Tony bent over her, his breath stinking of garlic. "The captain's gonna be right pleased to see you."

"So you want me alive." Kef said as one half of the handcuffs clicked around her wrist. "Big mistake."

She rolled to the side, yanking her arms down underneath her, pulling Tony down to the floor, tangling them both up in a mess of twisted limbs so interwoven the others didn't dare shoot. They grappled, rolling towards the bath, Tony's fingers digging into her hair and yanking her head back. He moved to elbow her throat but she ripped the knife from his belt and slammed it into his thigh, making him scream.

Squirming out from Tony's grip, she slapped a hand onto the bathtub. Before she could lever herself up, a boot crashed into her side, smashing the wind from her lungs. An arm wrapped around her chest, dragging her up, trying to rip her away from the bathtub. She managed to keep hold of the rim, but the movement toppled the tub, spilling scummy water across the floor. Her attacker slipped. Kef crashed down on top of him. Reedy and Max swung their batons and she caught one on the elbow, pain shooting up her bones, but the other crashed into her temple, sending light flashing behind her eyes.

That reminded her. The light. She had to reach it.

The batons came down again but Kef twisted sideways, sending the batons crunching into the man underneath her.

148

She tackled Reedy's legs, brought him staggering down, then she leapt up, the room and the guards spinning around her, still with a handcuff trailing from her left wrist. She swung it at another man as he closed in, knocking his baton away. Savage pride surged through Kef. It didn't last long before thick arms wrapped around her, pinning Kef's arms to her side.

She writhed, cursing, spittle foaming on her lips, boots slipping on the water below. His grip was too strong. The other four guards who were still standing rushed at her, batons smashing into her bones, stars exploding behind her eyes and the light bulb's glow pulsating bright and hideous above her. She tried doubling up, tried getting small, but the man behind her just laughed, and hauled her back up. As his muscled arms crushed her chest and the stench of his sweat overwhelmed her, Kef grinned a bloody smile.

Using his momentum, she flicked backwards, her legs spinning into the air above her, boots smashing into the light bulb and breaking the glass and the plaster ceiling in a shower of dust. The bulb fell from the hole, flickering out into darkness, sparks flying from the trailing power cord as the whole affair crashed down to the ground.

Down onto the water-soaked floor.

Guards screamed as electricity streaked through the water, spasming their bodies, making them splash onto the ground. Flesh cooked and hair burned. Electricity stabbed into Kef, but instead of shocking her, it soaked into her skin, filling her with adrenaline. Renewed by the energy, she staggered up, clutching the wall for support. Around her, bodies twitched. Dim light shone through the porthole, illuminating the mingled puddles of water and blood.

Her chest heaved. A few moments ago, she'd been yawning at the door. Now blood pumped through her so fast that Kef's heart felt like bursting, and every muscle throbbed with pain. The electricity helped, a little. Not enough. Damn, it'd been too long since she'd got a charge like that.

A boy screamed outside the room. Footsteps slapped away along the corridor, dragging the scream with them. Shit. She'd almost forgotten about Squine.

Kef grabbed a gun from a dead guard, then staggered towards the door, slamming it open with a thunderous bang. At the far end, Squine's webbed feet slid on the floor as he hurled himself down into the stairwell, his whimpers echoing along the corridor. Kef stumbled after him, bumping off the walls.

She slipped down the stairs, crashing onto the inn's floor below. Lightning flashed outside the ship, sending blue light stabbing through the portholes. Squine stood before one of those windows, panting and cursing while he tried to open it. Kef dragged herself up, baring her teeth.

With a rusty groan, the porthole inched open. Squine let out a nervous yelp, sliding his fingers into the gap to pry it wider.

Kef's legs wobbled. An animal growl rumbled in her chest. She lurched towards Squine, roaring, and Squine turned to look at her, halfway through opening the porthole, and if he'd been fast and brave enough he probably could've slipped out. But bravery in the face of Kef's anger took more courage than he'd ever possess.

He froze, white-faced and yellow-eyed. Kef crashed into him, smashing Squine's head against the porthole, slamming it shut, making him shriek. She threw his head against the porthole again, turning the shrieking into a whimpering gurgle, and then again and again until the glass shattered, spraying out into the midnight air.

Thunder shook the skies. A flash of lightning revealed the boy's face, all bloodied and cut, and Kef's own hands bloodier still. Rain sliced through the window. Wind howled.

"P-please!" Tears streaked down Squine's face, foam bubbling from his lips. "Master, p-please –"

She gripped his collar and yanked him up towards her, turning his begging into a fit of spluttering.

"Did you tell them the plan?" she growled.

"No!" Squine's yellow eyes widened, wet with tears. "No, I swear! And they don't know about Harold or Gabine either, I never mentioned them, I never wanted them to get caught up in this –"

"But you didn't care if I did."

Kef glared into his eyes. The boy looked away, swallowing. Plenty of fear there, but not a liar's fear. More like the fear of a kid knowing death was breathing heavy onto his face.

"I believe you," said Kef. "Too bad it doesn't matter anymore."

Thunder rumbled. Streaks of electricity flashed down to spear the Lightning Tower. Kef closed her eyes. The real storm wasn't the blaze and roar of lightning and thunder outside. It was the storm within. The shaking in her bones, the rage coursing through her veins. She wanted to let the storm consume her. But she bottled it with a snarl, because she couldn't unleash it until her task was done.

She opened her eyes, leaned down towards Squine, his collar still held in her fingers. "I know what it's like. To be scorned. To be a slave. To be caged. But I don't give a shit about that now, because there's only one end for anyone who betrays me."

Squine's quivered in her grip. His hands fell away from hers, and he grabbed a small object from his pocket. Lightning flashed, illuminating the locket held between his webbed fingers. So he'd had it all along.

"P-p-please!"

Kef pulled a knife from her belt, adjusted her grip. Such a shame. Such a waste. But she'd waste any number of lives to save her own, and that was a hard truth she'd long ago made peace with.

Squine's eyes squeezed shut. "No – no, please, I'm sorry, I'm sorry –"

"Open your eyes, you slimy little shit. At least die like a man."

But he kept his eyes closed, tears streaking out from under the lids. Damn it. She had half a mind to wrench those eyelids open, but she'd already delayed too long and there could be more guards on the way. Just a few days ago, Kef thought she could deal with Exoran without being corrupted by his filth. Looked like that was a foolish dream. All dreams were, in the end.

Kef plunged the knife underneath Squine's jaw, driving the blade in all the way to the crosspiece. Squine spasmed, eyelids rolling up, hand clenching around his locket, yellowed eyes gazing at the ceiling. Glassy. Sightless. One eyeball twitching.

She wrenched the knife out. She cleaned it on Squine's swimsuit, then shoved him through the porthole. He plunged into the sea in a messy splash that sent water bursting into the air.

Kef dragged a hand across her face, wiping away blood and rain and more besides. She limped to the exit. No storm inside her now. Just ragged breathing, shaky steps, and a terrible coldness making her shiver. With a red hand, she pushed the door open, leaving a bloody smear behind. Kef staggered along the dark corridor. Away from the inn. Away from the dead guards. Away from any hope of keeping herself above the filth.

Chapter 18: No Questions

G abine rolled over, groaning at the aching in her hip
as it pressed through the threadbare blankets and
against the cold metal floor. Her elbow bumped into
the railing. Wincing, she tucked it back by her side, staring
down through the void next to her. The empty seaweed silo
was dark, but there was a faint, dim blueness shining through
the tiny rivet-hole higher up the wall. From that blueness
she distinguished the water below, silky and black. It lapped
against the side walls with a faint ping. She closed her eyes,
hoping that listening to the ripples would lull her back to
sleep. If she tried hard enough, she could almost pretend the
pinging came from a distant piano, and that she was in the
great soaring chamber of Ivourium's concert hall, marvelling
at the Ascendant Orchestra communing with the divine ...

She'd been a light sleeper all her life. Her father said it was
because of her restless imagination. Her mother had snorted
and said it had more to do with her restless urge to annoy her
parents. Gabine was past seventy now, longer than either of
her parents had managed. It was strange how she still felt like
a child whenever she thought about them.

When it came to most other areas of life, she felt every one
of her seventy-two years, with some compound interest added

on for good measure. Did her own children still think about her? And if Alexi and Ryan did, did they think about her as a loving mother? Perhaps too focussed on her work, she was honest enough to admit, but still loving nonetheless, always there for her boys even if they hadn't shared the greatest deal of time together.

Or did they think of her the other way? The woman who'd gaped at the lawyers, not understanding why her husband wanted this, but still having to deal with it anyway because that's what she did with problems. Deal with them. Fix them. Move on. Her practicality helped her work, but she wished it could have been more useful in her personal life. Thankfully, she'd always had her work. What would she have done without it?

She rolled onto her back, fidgeting with the blankets, staring up at the ceiling. It was cheap steel, which would fold under an accidental strike from a large boat, but it was non-reactive and anti-corrosive. In essence, perfect for a storage silo. She shifted her gaze to the walkway above hers and counted all the bolt holds, imagining the engineering details drawn in her mind. That occupied her a little, but not as deeply as she wished.

Something splashed below. She froze. Was there something down in the water below? Or someone?

She rolled over, squinting to try and take in what little light there was. A body floated towards the ladder. A hand clasped the rungs, sending the walkway vibrating, and as the figure drew itself out from the water, Gabine opened her mouth, ready to scream.

The figure's head tilted back before Gabine could make a noise and the faint light revealed Kef's face, hair slicked against her skin. Gabine frowned. She thought she'd watched Kef slip away a while ago, along with Squine – who had yet to surface. However, in her foggy, sleep-deprived mind, she had supposed it to be a dream. Evidently, it was not. What had they been doing?

The metal trembled beneath Gabine as Kef clambered onto the walkway. She shook a glow cube. Yellow light flared from the object, making Gabine groan and press her eyelids together to supress the brightness. Beside her, Harold stirred, also moaning.

When Gabine opened her eyes, she wished she'd kept them shut. Kef stood five paces away, leaning on the railing, staring down at the rippling water below with a haunted look etched into her face. Blood smeared her clothes, cuts streaked across her face, and chunks had been ripped out of her hair.

Gabine swallowed. Was tonight when it happened? If that scowl was anything to judge by, perhaps Gabine's luck had reached an end.

"The giller betrayed us," said Kef in a hoarse voice.

"What?" asked Harold.

"He led me back to the inn. There were guards waiting for me."

"But we talked, he seemed like he could be trusted –"

"Well, he wasn't." Kef glared at them. "He betrayed me to the city guard. There's probably a bounty on my head, ever since I took you from the Factory, and Squine wanted to collect."

Kef swore. She drew a throwing knife from her belt, then hurled it across the silo at the corkboard target she'd set up earlier. It stabbed point-first into the cork, quivering. A perfect bullseye. Growling, Kef kicked the railing. The clang of metal reverberated around the silo. Gabine's heartbeat increased. Kef wore a charming mask, and most of the time she wore it so well Gabine thought there was nothing underneath.

In these last few days, however, there'd been moments when the mask had slipped. Now it was slipping away even further, revealing what Gabine glimpsed at Blackrake: a raging anger, bottled up inside Kef, waiting to be unleashed. Even at the prison ship, that anger hadn't fully escaped. Gabine shuddered to think what would happen when it did.

"What about the Lightning Tower?" she asked, trying to inject some steel into the shaky foundations of her voice.

Kef's glare turned towards her. "What about it?"

Gabine prayed that Kef's anger was directed solely towards Squine's betrayal. What if Squine hadn't betrayed her at all? What if Kef was simply using it as an excuse to get rid of the boy for annoying her? No, that didn't seem like Kef's style. Besides, if she wanted to kill them all, she wouldn't need an excuse. What could Gabine and Harold do to stop her?

"Well," said Gabine. "Without a giller, the plan won't work."

Kef's jaw clenched. "We'll have to adapt."

"Who will swim through the intake pipe, then?" asked Harold. "Do you have another giller?"

"I'll do his part instead," said Kef.

"That's impossible," said Gabine. "No one except a giller could manage it. In the first instance, you'll have to dive forty-five feet underwater –"

"There's no other choice."

"What about everything else?" asked Harold.

Kef was silent for a few moments while she stared at the drips falling off her clothes, splashing down into the water.

"As I said, we'll adapt."

She started talking about modifications to their plan, how

157

their roles would change, how everything they'd rehearsed would need rethinking. A small part of Gabine's mind marvelled at how quickly Kef was adjusting things, but the larger part of her was focussed on a singular fear; only in the last few hours had Gabine slotted the pieces together.

There was a reason Kef seemed to know the Lightning Tower so well, even before Gabine drew the plans. There was a reason Kef had been able to so easily cause havoc on Blackrake. Talking to Harold about their escape from the Alchemical Factory had only reinforced Gabine's suspicions.

Gabine sighed. Would things have been different, if she'd refused to build the Lightning Tower? Despite what she'd told Kef, she knew full well what the Channeler really was, even if she'd feigned ignorance and kept her office from knowing the full truth when they'd designed the Tower.

No objections. That lesson was drummed into Gabine from the first day of her apprenticeship. You were never designing for yourself, but always for the client, and if that meant you felt uneasy about the work, that was all part of the job. After all, what responsibility did you really have? If you refused, someone else with looser morals and lower budgets would fill your place.

No questions, apart from anything beyond the logistics. That was how you made your clients happy. That was how she'd built her masterpieces, won her awards, grown her studio, recruited her apprentices, and chipped away at her morals. When she looked back, it seemed obvious how it happened. At the time, however, it had been so gradual, so slow, and she had only grasped the truth when it was too late.

Gabine thought about all the rich clients who had used her services. Half of the conversations seem to revolve around where to put the feeding trays for their specially bred cats. All her wealthy clients thought they were uniquely sophisticated and special, but she had seen through them easily enough. Their boats weren't for sailing across the water, impressing their friends, or making their rivals envious. They were for settling the deep unease inside them. The unease that came when you had everything you ever wanted, only to discover that up close the gold was little more than a gilded veneer.

And so they asked Gabine to design pleasure cruisers to rival city-ships, hoping that it would let them recreate themselves as well. Gabine had pitied them. Still, she'd accepted their money without asking any uncomfortable questions. How strange that she'd become like them, now. Except for the richness. The irony was laughable. She had none of their wealth, but she shared the same life of hollow accomplishments, and now she was about to destroy her greatest legacy.

"So, there's our plan," said Kef. "Any questions, Gabine?"

Gabine looked up, startled out of her reverie. Kef looked at her, expectant. There was a frown on Kef's face, but her anger had been tucked back away behind her façade. Gabine exhaled a pent-up breath. It looked like she'd be surviving for now. As much as she didn't want to admit it, that was all Gabine really cared about these days. What had happened to the girl who'd dreamed of cities shining with light, spires soaring into the air, boats more graceful than the waves themselves?

The same thing that happened to every girl, in the end. She'd grown up.

"No," said Gabine. "No questions."

Chapter 19: Sign of the Past

As he worked, Harold watched the water at the silo's base. It was still. Still and dark. Harold sighed. Most of the time, he was cheerful, because life was too short for sadness.

Even worrying about his wife's reaction to his apparent kidnapping hadn't bothered him for long. Mainly, that was because Mina knew about Kef. Once she put the pieces together, her panic would be quelled, although she would still act worried for the city guard's benefit.

And beyond that, the chaos of Harold's escape had been dwarfed by reuniting with Kef. When Kef said why she needed his help, it had filled him with a powerful sense of purpose, knowing they were about to right a great wrong.

But as he gazed down at the water where Squine should have been, Harold found it difficult to muster that same righteousness. Was he simply nervous about tomorrow's mission, or did his queasiness speak to something else?

Harold finished coating the plastic strip with the chemical paste. He took another sheet of plastic, then stuck it over the other strip, sealing the paste between the layers to create a chemtab. He put the strip down, making sure to keep it away from the others he'd made. Alone, the chemtabs were perfectly inert. But if two pairs of chemtabs were peeled apart, then stuck together, it would create anything from a poisonous gas to an acidic solution that could burn through metal, depending on what chemicals he'd included.

Harold turned to Kef. "Squine didn't deserve this."

Kef looked up from the back of her hand, where she was drawing patterns onto her skin with a marker. She'd borrowed it from Gabine, who was on the far side of the silo, mulling over her plans.

Kef scowled. "No one deserves anything."

"He was a nice boy."

"Who tried to get me killed."

"He liked a girl, you know, and she –"

"Don't bother. He already told me that sob story."

"Kef, maybe he tried to kill you, but it wasn't all his fault."

"Then whose fault was it?"

"Zorith. The Kazzia. This whole system we've created to drive gillers into slavery –"

"I've been through worse." Kef glared. "And I'd never sell out someone like that. Neither would you."

That was true. Even as a tiny malnourished scrap of a girl, there'd been a streak of toughness about Kef when Harold found her under the covers of his dingy, hiding from the city guard. It was something in her eyes. They were a striking blue, holding an intensity far beyond her years. After he'd taken her in, he'd discovered she was only fourteen. Somehow, she looked both older and younger at the same time.

There was little similarity between that girl and the woman who sat before him now. Kef had grown tall and strong, with her pale skin turned golden and tanned by fifteen years sailing the Twisted Seas. Still, one thing hadn't changed since he'd

161

met Kef. Once she set her mind on a goal, it happened, and she didn't let anyone stand in her way.

"This city isn't evil," Harold said. "There are good people here."

"And?"

"I'm worried about what we're doing."

Kef's grip tightened around her pen, making her knuckles turn white. Harold stared calmly at her.

She sagged, all the rage in her body deflating in an instant. All her years vanished, and Harold was looking again at the scared little girl who'd needed his help.

"I can't do this without you," she said.

"You won't have to. I'm not leaving."

A smile creased her hawkish face. She sat up straighter.

"I'm just worried that you care less about justice and more about revenge," he said.

Her smile vanished, replaced with a hard scowl. "They're the same thing."

"We just need to consider how –"

"No! Everyone in this city-ship profits from the Tower. Everyone's guilty, even if they don't know it. Especially if they don't. You don't get it, do you? This isn't about laws or rules or *negotiating*. I know what you've been up to over the last few years, with your teaching and your campaigning and your charity. What has that ever achieved? A few more kids rescued from the slums to train as alchemists? A few gillers weaned off addictions, but only after being slaves for twenty years? You can't make a game fair when it's rigged from the start. It has to be destroyed. And if that means violence and riots and pain, then that's what we're going to create."

Kef leaned forward. "Are you in? Or are you out?"

Harold's head spun. How had she known about all of that? The apprenticeships he'd granted to underprivileged children was public knowledge, but Harold thought his wife was the only one who knew about everything else he'd done.

Kef had inspired it. After he'd nursed her back to full health, keeping her hidden in his houseboat, he'd smuggled her onto a cargo ship and helped her escape from Zorith. For a few years, the glow of his secret rebellion had granted him a quiet assurance that he'd done something to be truly proud of. The feeling had been far more satisfying than the awards and commendations he'd received as an alchemist. Then he'd realised there was so much wrong with the world. One act of charity was not nearly enough.

Despite acting as a rule-abiding alchemist, he'd done everything he could to help those suffering. He'd created alchemical solutions to wean gillers and wingers off the Zetamyre that kept them addicted and in debt, even long after they'd escaped their indentured servitude. He'd created supplements for wingers to help them deal with the pains of growing their wings, and now those supplements had circulated throughout the Twisted Seas. He had campaigned to raise the wages of the gillers who served the Alchemical Guild as security workers, and he'd won. And he did all this without anyone knowing he was the one behind it, because if the Guild knew, they'd fire him for daring to usurp their business, and then he'd no longer have the resources to help at all.

Even after all that he'd done, a sick feeling squirmed inside Harold as he sat before Kef. Had he really tried everything he could? Most of his waking hours were dedicated to alchemy – to the projects his managers set him, to solving the problems of rich clients, and to his own fascinations. Was it wrong, for

163

a man to see injustice in the world, and not dedicate all his power towards fixing it?

And when it came to it, had he truly cared about the people he'd freed from their oppression, or had he just wanted that warm glow of satisfaction? Had he just wanted people to remark on how happy he was? How self-assured and jovial and kind and compassionate he always seemed to be? Had he just wanted his wife to say he was a good man?

In the final analysis, he'd done a lot of good, whatever his reasons were. However, when it came to the Lightning Tower, he'd known the truth about it for fifteen years. Yet he'd never thought of anything that could fix it. Now he realised that was because he couldn't solve the problem from working inside the Alchemists' Guild.

But Kef wasn't on the inside. She had no rules, no boundaries, and maybe that was exactly what was needed.

"I'm in," he said.

"Good."

There was no smile from her. No sense of approval; simply a businesslike sense of purpose. Once, that might have irked Harold, given the risks he was taking. Now, he found that he didn't care. His feelings weren't important. What mattered was the mission, and the thought of that brought a warm glow that seemed brighter than any other act of charity he'd done.

Kef held up the back of her left hand. The rest of her skin was well-tanned from a life of sailing, but the back of her left hand was freckled and pale. On the skin, she'd drawn a strange marking.

"Remember the tattoo I had? I need a way to remove it from someone else." She chewed her lip. "Quickly, and with less pain. And then I also need a way to ink it onto several other

164

people."

The back of Harold's neck prickled. He remembered screams, stifled by a rag stuffed into Kef's mouth, and the acrid smell of burning flesh. On her hand, Kef had drawn this marking with a felt-tipped pen, so it would wash off in the water. The original tattoo, however, had not been as simple to remove. Fortunately, Harold's skill had progressed somewhat in the last fifteen years.

"Can you do it?" she asked.

Harold nodded. "I can."

Chapter 20: Evening Pleasantries

Nicholas Patrick Bartholomew simply failed to understand the opera. As he sat in the upper gallery, Lady Francine Belleville oohing and aahing beside him, he pressed the back of his fine-fingered hand to his mouth, stifling a yawn. On the stage far below, the diva's aria rose to a quavering pitch, the noise thrumming in the back of Nicholas' throat. If only he'd remembered his earplugs.

He contented himself with the fact that, when he ruled Zorith, he would not sully himself with attending the opera. Desperate to follow his example, soon no one else would, either. Although High Captain Exoran was missing as usual, and there was still a packed house, so maybe the trend would be too difficult to change …

Perhaps the opera was a necessary burden for the upper crust of Zorith. At least it let Nicholas display his well-tailored suits and even more well-chosen dates to the people who really mattered in this city.

The aria rose to an ear-splitting pitch. Nicholas' gaze flicked down to his champagne flute, wondering if the shrill singing would break the glass. Alas, the aria ended without even that small concession to excitement. The crowd applauded. Nicholas clapped along with them. When he saw the first hint of a standing ovation beginning to form, he stood too, and an appreciative "oooh" came from Lady Belleville beside him. Soon the whole room was on their feet. Beaming from the stage below, the diva bowed low to her audience. The applause grew louder. Clenching his jaw, Nicholas increased his efforts. When one sought to climb, one was not choosy about the rungs used for the task.

Golden chandeliers illuminated the grand theatre. Rich velvet curtains fluttered across the stage. With a sudden outburst of chatter, everyone began to leave.

"Oh, darling!" Lady Belleville's white-gloved hands wrapped around Nicholas' arm and he did his best not to flinch. "Wasn't that simply wonderful?"

Simple was one word for it.

"I thought it was marvellous!" said Nicholas. "Why, that singer at the end near brought a tear to my eye!"

A tear of disgust, perhaps.

Lady Belleville fluttered her eyelashes at him. "Oh, darling, I am so glad you enjoyed it!"

She held tight to Nicholas as they swanned down the grand, red-carpeted steps of the theatre. Other high-class men and women bumped against them as they exited onto the deck of a neighbouring ship. Overlooking the glittering expanse of Zorith, the *Meridian Cruiser's* deck was filled with fine restaurants, pleasure gardens, and more than a few hidden alcoves occupied by giggling couples. Judging by the hot little breaths Lady Belleville was exhaling into Nicholas' ear, she was keen to explore those alcoves herself.

He'd have to find some excuse to avoid that. She was a nice lady, and quite pretty, but even if he were attracted to women, Nicholas wouldn't want tonight going any further than a polite peck on the cheek. Lady Belleville was someone to be seen with, and that was all. With her hanging off his arm, it would be easier to court women of a status just above her, and then once he'd been seen with them, he'd move to the women above them. When your station was as low as Nicholas' had been, you needed every advantage you could get to rise to the top.

"Shall we get some canapes?" he asked, pointing to a small bar at the ship's prow, with a wonderful view over Zorith's harbour.

Lady Belleville cast a longing look at a giggling trio who were skipping towards a shadowy grotto in the pleasure gardens. "I'd love to, darling."

Nicholas strode towards the bar, Lady Belleville on his arm. A few envious gazes turned his way. He smiled to some of his watchers, waved politely to others, and ignored the rest. Ah, this was living! To be known amongst the best of society, and to be climbing towards his long-cherished dream of power and influence.

A tuxedoed waiter bowed as they approached the bar. "Do you have a reservation, sir and madam?"

Behind the waiter, a rope separated the rest of the boat from the prow section, where ten stools carved from the finest mondoceros-ivory were arranged beside the railing, offering an incredible view of the harbour below, with all the lights of the boats twinkling like fireflies.

"I most certainly do," said Nicholas.

He stuck a hand into his breast-pocket to retrieve the cream-coloured reservation card. Dampness greeted his fingers. Flinching, he withdrew his hand from the pocket, pulling out a small scrap of ragged paper. It read:

The Rupez-Corsen Clock Tower. Ten o'clock. – K.

His heartbeat gave an excited flutter. K was the spy he'd met in *Flagship Augustine*, the night of Exoran's first party. As promised, Nicholas had used a courier to deliver regular reports about Zorith's nobility over the last few days. This, however, was the first he'd heard back from her. She must have been highly impressed with his work!

Except ... there was a possibility it might be the opposite. A sudden coldness filled him, colder even than that time when a wave had knocked him off his uncle's yacht. What if K was dissatisfied with his performance? At this time of night, the Rupez-Corsen Clock Tower was not well-frequented. It would be the perfect location for an unwitting gentleman to be accosted by brigands.

"Darling?" A frown creased Lady Belleville's powdered face. "Do you have the reservation?"

Nicholas glanced at his wristwatch. Twenty minutes until ten o'clock. It would take fifteen to reach the Rupez-Corsen Clock Tower. He gulped. K wouldn't take kindly to ignoring her message. He could hardly claim ignorance, either. Someone had slipped that message into his pocket while they exited the theatre, he was sure of it! That same person might be watching him even now.

Nicholas took a deep breath. He was certain he had done well. No other spy would have deduced that Lady Clementine was having an affair with a winger from the city guard, or that Lord Cristo's wealth came from an illegal gambling den in Zorith's filthy slums.

Yes, this meeting was surely to reward him. On the small chance it wasn't ... well, K had the resources to find him anyway. Not that punishment was a possibility. No, certainly not! Most likely she was about to promote him to a new position – and what fantastic timing, given that at the Lightning Tower tomorrow night, High Captain Exoran would announce his new governors.

Nicholas bent over, raising Lady Belleville's hand to his lips. "I am most sorry for this, my lady, but I have realised that I have an urgent appointment to be getting to."

Lady Belleville gaped, her red lips sparkling in the night-time light. Next to them, the tuxedoed waiter shuffled a few steps backwards, fading away. Lady Belleville's tinted eyebrows furrowed into a dangerous-looking shape and she opened her mouth to rage at him.

"I wish I could stay with you, my lady." Nicholas raised his hands in a pacifying gesture. "Unfortunately, this summons comes from one of the High Captain's governors."

"Oh!" That frown vanished, her forehead returning to a smooth, unwrinkled state. "The High Captain … that's very exciting, darling! Please, do let me know how it goes."

She gave a coy smile and rubbed his arm. Nicholas smiled back.

"I will," he lied.

#

By the winds of the sea, he hadn't expected this to be so difficult.

Nicholas scowled at the puddle stretching across the walk-way, then glanced down at his gloriously expensive leather shoes. He sighed. Where was a servant when you needed them?

Wincing, he tiptoed across the walkway, cursing the indignity. He hadn't descended this deep into Zorith since he was a child! With the flickering lamps, shanty-boats all jumbled against each other, and unsavoury characters moaning in dark corners, it was no place for a gentleman to grace with his presence. He hoped Exoran rewarded him for his sacrifice.

Nicholas reached the rendezvous location: a small pontoon with a tall steel clock tower rising from the centre. Judging by the unpleasantly dark stains splattered around the ground, and an equally unpleasant odour, the commoners used this place for one of their disgusting meat markets. High up on the clocktower, a ghastly gargoyle surveyed the whole scene. Nicholas sniffed. The taste of these people was appalling!

He glanced around. No sign of K, but there were still a few minutes until their appointed meeting time. He stood with his back to the clock tower, shoving his hands into the pockets of his well-tailored pants to stave off the bitter wind sweeping across the sea. He shivered. Perhaps this suit was stylish, but it certainly wasn't warm.

Distant music and laughter drifted from the *Meridian Cruiser*, where he'd left Lady Belleville. He squinted towards the ship. From here, it seemed so tall and far away, and so very bright compared to the dark districts he'd walked through. He leaned forward, somehow hoping that would let him hear more of the ship's noise. Instead, the wind shifted and all he heard was the rusty groaning of the shanty-boats around his little pontoon.

Removing his hands from his pockets, he rubbed them together, like he'd seen some of the city guards do on night patrol. Oh, what he would give to be warm in his cabin, looking out over Zorith through his porthole window, instead of being trapped in the city itself. Zorith was so much prettier from a distance.

Where was K? It was almost time to meet, and she didn't strike Nicholas as someone who arrived late. There was a hard-headed efficiency about her that was strangely alluring, even despite Nicholas' tastes.

More importantly than the matter of her arrival, there was another issue to resolve. How should he be standing? Definitely not with his hands in his pockets, he realised, feeling sheepish. Leaning against the clock tower would project an air of swaggering confidence, but perhaps the casualness would make her think he was unsuited to a role in the High Captain's government. Instead, he stood with his arms folded behind his back. Stoic. Imperious. Ready for anything this city would throw at him.

A gentle patter of water fell against his face, making him splutter. Lightning flashed in the distance. A few seconds later, the boom of thunder rattled Nicholas' bones. The rain grew heavier, streaking down his face and flattening his carefully brill-creamed hair. Scowling, he tried to flick it back into a better shape. If only he'd brought an umbrella.

Above him, a dull gong sounded from the clock tower. Ten o'clock.

A circle of rope dropped over Nicholas, landing with a splash around his feet.

"Huh?"

The rope constricted, slamming his ankles together, tightening against his skin, making him sprawl onto the horribly dirty ground. It yanked at his ankles, hauling his legs up into the air. His head crashed into the clock tower's side and then he was ascending, upside down, the ground vanishing beneath him and his stomach churning. He screamed. The rope dragged him up past the clockface, which was still donging from the hour's striking. Nicholas' screech grew louder. He was going to be dragged into the sky, into the storm clouds above –

Everything went weightless. He kept shooting up for a brief moment, and then gravity yanked down on him, dragging him back towards the ground. His eyes widened and he flapped madly with his arms, as if that would somehow stop his fall, but then the rope caught firm. It jerked him around, swinging and twisting and blurring Zorith's lights. He closed his eyes, yelling for someone to save him.

A hand clamped over his mouth, stopping his swinging, stifling his scream. Nicholas' heart thudded. Trembling, he opened his eyes, feeling woozy from the blood rushing to his head.

The gargoyle standing atop the clock tower gazed back at him. Its hand left his mouth to grab his jacket's collar.

"Oh god!" he whimpered, shivering from the piercing rain. "Oh god!"

The gargoyle shrugged. "Close enough."

Lightning flashed through the air, illuminating the gargoyle's face. Except it wasn't the gargoyle. It was K. Dressed in a battered cloak, the cowl over her head to fend off the rain, but unmistakably the spy who'd summoned Nicholas. Although, if the scowl on her face was anything to go by, Nicholas would have preferred to deal with a gargoyle brought to life.

"Have you betrayed me, Nicholas?" asked K.

"N-n-no!" Tears streaked down Nicholas' forehead, mingling with the rain lashing against his face. "N-n-no, I would never, I swear I would never –"

"I know." K leaned forward, baring her teeth, sending hot breath washing over his face. "Keep it that way."

Nicholas bobbed his head. His chest strained from the hammering of his heart. Was she going to let him down?

"You've done well with your reports," she said.

173

"Th-thank you."

"May our ships float forever."

K released his collar. Nicholas swung away from her and his heart skipped a beat. A fresh wave of nausea swelled through him and his mouth went dry, too dry to scream, and as he swung out over the void, the rope slipped, dropping him. He screwed up his face and his stomach clenched and he thought that this was the end of it all. But then he swung back to K and she clutched his lapels.

"May our ships float f-f-forever," Nicholas said.

"Take these." She pressed a plastic bag into his shaking hands. "And listen to what I'm about to say like your life depends on it."

Chapter 21: Old Wounds

Kef watched Nicholas stumble up from the ground. He loosened the rope she'd used to lower him, then scurried away from the pontoon, vanishing into the darkness. She nodded. A stuck-up idiot if there ever was one, but Nicholas could follow orders. His role in tomorrow's mission was safe.

She sighed. Watching him squirm had been refreshing, but now that he was scurrying away, a heavy melancholy sank its claws into Kef. That stupid giller ... why had Squine forced her to kill him? Once the mission was done, she might've even freed him from the Kazzia. Damn it, she'd shown him kindness, hadn't she? And he'd thrown it away!

Brightness flashed from the Lightning Tower's spire. Thunder boomed, cutting through the rain's pounding. Beneath Kef, the clocktower swayed. Harsh seas tonight. Not a good time to be caught on the open ocean. But she'd rather be out there, dealing with the raging storm, if it meant she could've avoided this mess in Zorith.

She drew in a rattling breath, gazing at the Lightning Tower. Keep it together for another day. That's all she had to do. Then her job was done and she might feel a measure of peace.

Another spear of lightning flashed towards the tower. She

stretched a hand towards the lightning, squinting so that it looked like she was pinching it between finger and thumb. But within an eyeblink, it was gone. Like life, really. Brief and torturous, glorious for maybe a moment, but never forever.

She climbed down the tower. Her boots splashed in puddles as she stepped onto the pontoon. Kef trudged sternwards, hunched over to keep dry from the rain. Her boot clanked onto the walkway. She paused. Turning, she looked over her shoulder at the sign above another path, pointing to a familiar district.

She had to return to the silo to rest before tomorrow's heist. But before then, she had a few hours. Two, maybe three. And she was close enough to the place, so what harm could it do?

Pivoting on her bootheel, she strode towards the other jetty. She clanked along walkways and pontoons, moving through patches of darkness and light. Everything swayed underneath her. Water chopped against the walkways, spraying fresh coldness onto her skin. No guards out tonight, most likely on the rain's account. She was grateful for that much.

Kef rounded a corner and there it was: a squat houseboat that floated beside the walkway. A mural of a giant purple squid painted on the hull distinguished it from the drabber neighbouring boats, and golden light shone through seams in the shuttered windows. Kef paused, licking her lips.

Without conscious thought, her legs moved her towards the rear door, which was six paces from the walkway, connected by a narrow plank. A strange looseness flooded Kef's muscles. She'd never really had much choice when it came to Antoinette, had she? Not that she'd minded.

Over the years, Kef had returned to Zorith frequently, assessing the city-ship, thinking about the Lightning Tower, and trying to figure out how she could get inside. On one of those trips, she'd met Antoinette.

Kef had never wanted it to be more than a one-night stand, but on her next visit she wasn't entirely disappointed to repeat the experience. A few days every few years, that was all they'd shared. Still, it had made Kef eager for her regular scouting trips.

Usually, she slipped a note into Antoinette's house to ask her out for drinks. But tonight there was no time for the courtesy of a note.

Kef crossed the plank, timber creaking under her boots. She reached the door. No shutters over this one, just a sturdy metal hatch, a small porthole with a curtain drawn across the inside, blurring the boat's interior into a wash of warm light. Kef raised a trembling hand, ready to knock.

The curtain drew aside. A girl stared at Kef, her brow furrowed in a puzzled expression. She looked no older than five. Kef frowned. Wrong address?

The girl's head tilted to the side and recognition slammed into Kef. A heart-shaped face. Eyebrows with a strange kink in the middle, formed into tiny Vs. That lopsided quirk on the left side of her mouth. Like Antoinette, just in miniature.

"Hello," said the girl.

A lump formed in Kef's throat. She glanced past the girl, into the corridor. There was that flute, hanging from a wall bracket. There was that green bandana tied around it, covered in dust. But there were also things she didn't recognise. Picture frames. Odd knick-knacks. Grubbiness on the walls, smeared by small hands.

"What do you want?" asked the little girl.

Damn it, she even sounded like Antoinette.

"Nothing," whispered Kef. "There's nothing I want."

She turned away, stuffing her hands into her pockets, then stalked off into the night.

Chapter 22: What Drives a Man

High Captain Robert Exoran removed his reading optics and rubbed his eyes, groaning. With a yawn, he replaced his optics and squinted at the requisition document, adjusting his desk lamp to throw more light across the paper.

Rain lashed against the windows. Lightning flashed outside, but his insulated walls dampened the thunder. Not by much. Zorith was perpetually noisy. For a city independent of prana oil, it was a price you paid – and not the only one. Not the only one by a long way.

All those sacrifices had hurt him, over the years. To see the pain he'd caused to strangers and friends, lovers and family – it would have broken a lesser man. There'd been times when he'd wanted to rip the Lightning Tower and the city apart and start over completely, but he'd resigned himself to accepting the struggles of keeping Zorith operational. That's what leadership was. To make the hard sacrifices others wouldn't, to put the many ahead of the few, and to take the burden of guilt upon your shoulders so that everyone else could live in blissful ignorance.

On the requisition form, letters wriggled and twisted, skipping away whenever he looked at them. He rubbed his eyes again, trying to focus. All around his office, portraits of former High Captains glared down at him, as if they were embarrassed by his fatigue.

"Jeremy?" he called. "Could you please come in here to read this?"

His secretary didn't respond. Exoran remembered that he'd already sent the man home. How had he forgotten?

Exoran glanced at the clock. It was an antique that displayed its mechanisms behind a glass case, given to him on his fifteenth birthday by his grandmother. It took Exoran a while to process the clock's numbers. When he did, he gaped. How could it already be two in the morning?

He pushed himself up, wincing as his back made a popping noise. All this reading was stooping his posture. He blinked away a surge of light-headedness as he shuffled to the counter for coffee, trying to ignore the stares of former high captains, and the papers stacked three feet high on his desk. You could barely see the wood underneath.

It took forever to brew the coffee and after the first sip he wondered if it was worth the effort. Definitely not up to Jeremy's standards. He could see the man now, chuckling and shaking his head at Exoran's pitiful attempt.

Exoran stared out the porthole as he drank. The Lightning Tower flashed every few seconds as bolts struck the spire, illuminating the glass domed room at the top. Tomorrow night – no, tonight, because it was already two in the morning – that room would be full of people clamouring to be part of his government. Not Zorith's bravest, not Zorith's best, but simply the people who'd weaselled, blackmailed, and bred their way to the top. As it stood, only the hope of joining Exoran's government had stopped them protesting his ousting of High Captain Callaghan. If Exoran picked enough of the right people to join his government, those protests would never materialise. Get it wrong, however, and Zorith could face its second revolt in as many weeks.

Exoran took another sip, rubbing his eyes. Leadership was about sacrifice. He'd known that when he'd joined the Navy. He'd known that when he agreed to oversee the Lightning Tower, despite full knowledge of the lie it housed. And he'd especially known about the sacrifices in store for him when he'd overthrown the former High Captain.

Exoran sighed. Callaghan was a good woman. He was glad he'd granted her exile instead of execution. His younger self would have made a different choice, but the years had taught him temperance. A little kindness could prove more effective than a stick, so long as it was used judiciously.

He hoped Callaghan wasn't taking exile too hard. She was decent, he'd give her that, but she wasn't strong, and with the threats Exoran knew were coming, Zorith needed strength. Harsh men for harsh times. A painful reality, but such was the sacrifice of war.

Someone knocked at the door. Exoran jerked, almost spilling his coffee onto a marble bust of Robert McVeigh, the first High Captain of Zorith. He set his cup on the counter. A fresh burst of rain splattered against the portholes.

"Who is it?" he asked.

"It's us!"

A lump formed in his throat. Exoran strode to the door, fresh energy surging through his limbs. He threw open the door then crouched to hug his daughter. Clarice hugged him back. She felt so wonderfully warm.

"Are you almost done, Daddy?"

"Almost."

There was wetness in his eyes. He dragged a hand across them, wiping the wetness away before his girl could see them. It had been a hard week. He'd lost friends, exiled more, killed men and women he'd once called allies. Hardest of all, though, was how little time he had spent with his family.

He released Clarice, then stood to hug his son, who slouched beside his daughter. Owen put down the parcel he was holding, then returned the hug a little reluctantly, not as earnest as Clarice, but it was still enough to make Exoran's smile widen.

"Where's your mother?" he asked.

"Sleeping," said Owen.

Exoran frowned. "You didn't come here alone, did you?"

"No, Captain Willy took us. He's outside." Clarice pointed at the door behind her, then her face slackened when she saw Exoran frown at the door. "He's not in trouble, is he? It was our idea, not his –"

"You're not in trouble. Neither is William. I just wanted to make sure you weren't wandering off on your own."

Owen rolled his eyes. "Dad, no one else on this ship is even awake right now."

It wasn't people on this ship Exoran worried about. There had been far too much unrest in Zorith since his takeover. On just this Kailisday gone, there'd been an explosion and a kidnapping at the Alchemical Factory, attributed to the work of a Blackrake Prison escapee.

When Warden Henderson arrived in Zorith a few days ago, he'd promised to hunt the fugitive with utmost discretion. Exoran had given him permission, but after that disaster at the Factory, he'd sent Henderson back to Blackrake. The last thing he needed was a trigger-happy Warden causing chaos around Zorith. Exoran's own city guards would be more than capable of capturing the fugitive by themselves, and far less disruptive.

Clarice hoisted the parcel into the air, beaming. "We brought you this!"

Exoran took the package, trying to forget about the chaos swirling through his head. He unwrapped it, revealing a tray filled with cookies. The mouth-watering scent of fresh baking filled Exoran's nose, making his stomach rumble. How long since he'd last eaten?

"Clarice made us do it," said Owen, looking down at the floor. "Woke me up, as well –"

She nudged his hip. "You weren't sleeping either!"

"Yeah, but I –"

"Owen. Clarice." Exoran raised one to his lips, inhaling the smell, then took a bite. "These are delicious."

Clarice's smile grew even wider as she bounced up and down on her heels, her pigtails flapping against her back. Even Owen let a slight smile creep across his surly face. The cookies really were wonderful. Still warm and gooey, the chocolate buds almost turning to liquid as they touched his tongue. Much nicer than his bitter coffee.

Clarice peered around Exoran's legs, looking into the office. "Can we help?"

"You have." He kissed her forehead. "Now go back to sleep. I'll be home soon."

Once he'd said goodbye, he stepped back into the office, then locked the door. He managed to stumble to the counter and put down the cookies before he bent over and cried. It was all too much. Leading Zorith, betraying Callaghan, dealing with the riots, and now his own daughter and son so desperate to see him that they couldn't sleep, and still he'd turned them away after a few paltry moments. What kind of father was he?

Maybe he should give up. Pack his family onto his yacht, throw the High Captain's hat into the crowd of greedy honourborns, then sail into the sunset. He had enough money to keep them content for a dozen lifetimes. And if it came to it, he'd always liked the idea of fishing ...

No. He drew in a firm breath, grabbed the edge of his desk, then rose. Lightning flashed outside, basking the room in a white glow.

Neglecting his family hurt. It hurt more than any pain he'd endured before. But he had vowed to bear whatever weight was necessary to keep the city-ship afloat. If that meant accepting the weight of the whole world, then so be it.

He grabbed the cookies, then strode over to his desk, sitting down in the chair that had held so many leaders. Exoran didn't believe in ghosts, but he liked to imagine the former High Captains were with him as he grabbed the nearest document and started reading, a pen in one hand, his daughter's cookie in the other.

Tonight. The ball at the Lightning Tower would decide Zorith's future. Pick the right people to join his government, and maybe Zorith would be saved. Pick poorly and everything would be lost. He was drowsy, he was starving, and he was missing his family with more anguish than he'd ever felt before, but he would continue to sacrifice himself if that saved Zorith. Because that's what leaders did.

DAYS OF THE WEEK

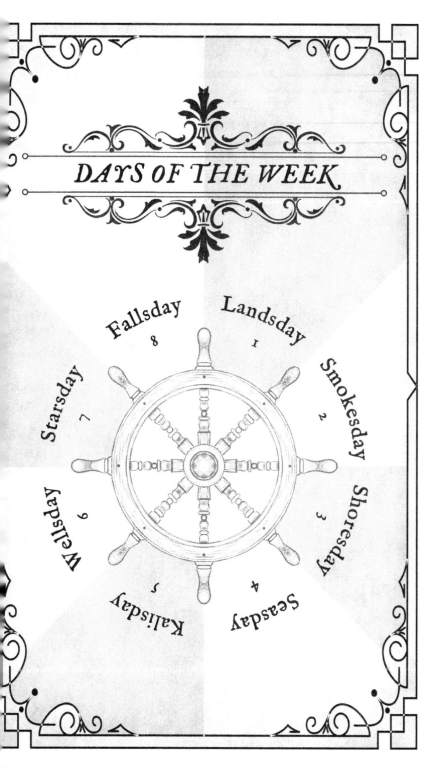

Fallsday 8

Landsday 1

Starsday 7

Smokesday 2

Shoresday 3

Wellsday 6

Seasday 4

Kalisday 5

Chapter 23: Grindhouse

As Tully looked down at the corpse barge, he wrinkled his nose. Gillers always smelled the worst.

"Did you have to get the Slimer?" he asked the barge driver, sticking out a finger to point at the giller sprawled amongst the tangled corpses.

The bargewoman shrugged. "Policy's policy."

"Policy's a pain in the arse," Tully muttered.

Using the crane, Tully hauled the corpse crate inside the grindhouse boat. The machinery groaned. Lot of rain early tonight, probably filled the thing up. Why hadn't the bloody bargewoman emptied it out, eh? With a shudder of metal, Tully placed the crate down on the tracks, neat as you'd please. He wasn't good at much, Tully knew, but he had a good hand with cranes.

With a puttering of her engine and a stinking cloud of petrol-smoke, the bargewoman's boat chugged off into the night. Tully gave her the finger. Good riddance. The bargewoman thought she was so special, but anyone could collect corpses. Turning them into something useful was an art. Tully's art.

He rolled the crate along the tracks, humming to himself. No one else around to bother him during night shift, just the way he liked. People were a nuisance. Better dead, when they

187

didn't talk.

Tully heaved against the crate's latches, opening the container and spilling corpses onto the ground. He stripped off their clothes, cutting them with his knife where things were tangled. The boss didn't like chopped clothes because they were harder to sell, but the boss also said be fast. So Tully had jumped through that, whaddaya call it, loophole.

Once their clothes were off, he heaved the naked corpses onto the conveyer belt, then slammed the start button. Groaning and clanking, the belt started up. Further into the grindhouse a washer would clean the bods, and then the conveyer belt tipped the corpses in a big open-topped funnel filled with whirring metal teeth. By the time Tully got the second-last body on the belt, the grinder was already chewing into flesh and bone, squeezing tubes of pink meat out into the box at the end. If someone else was here, they'd probably gag at the smell. Maybe puke. A new kid did that last week. Tully had hardened to the smell over the years. Probably helped that ever since working here, he hadn't eaten meat.

Tully looked down at the last bod. The giller. Still hadn't gotten to coping with that stench. Alive they smelled bad, but dead they smelled worse than a whale carcass dried in the sun for a month. And that ain't no fib, 'cause last year he fed twenty tons of whale blubber into the grinder, chopped into hundred-kilo pieces at a time.

The giller's slitted yellow eyes stared up at Tully. Water still leaked from the gaping wound under his chin, and his shoulders and neck were slashed something bad. His hands were clenched into fists. No peaceful end for this kid. But who got peaceful ends, anyway? Not as many as most folk thought, Tully knew. And he really knew. Working with corpses had taught him a lot of things, and in some ways he knew more about these folk dead than others knew about them alive. Could always separate the lucky ones who died of age and time from the ones who'd parted the world ugly and butchered. This giller kid was the latter. Must've pissed someone off bad.

Didn't want to smear that giller smell over him, so Tully fired up a crane. Tongue pressed against the gap in his teeth, Tully lowered the hook onto the giller's chest, then led it up his body, scraping against the scales, until it caught under the kid's chin in that knife-hole. Tully smiled. Got it on the first try.

The crane yanked the giller up by his head, arms and legs dangling to show off those webbed toes that made Tully shudder. It was a relief to drop the corpse onto the conveyer belt.

Tully stretched, yawning. Once that last bod was minced up good, he just had to take the meat crate into cold storage and then his work was done. Kill a few hours, then the shift was over and he'd go to *Cock's Crow* for some well-deserved relaxing. Maybe *Madam Silk's* if he was feeling flush. Not that he had much left after betting against Eriss in the Naumachia. The giller woman couldn't stop winning.

Over from the grinder came a horrible shrieking. Cursing, Tully slammed the emergency stop, then ran towards the machine. Must be the kid. Just like a giller to screw things up.

Tully peered down into the grinder as the blood-soaked mincing cogs spun to a stop. Gristle quivered in the machine and the stench of chopped giller made Tully's nose twitch.

Something gleamed down in the machine's guts. Tully frowned. Was that a ring? He crossed over to the tool bench,

189

picked up the extendable grabber hand, then stomped back to the grinder. Where had the giller been keeping that ring? Up his arse?

Huffing, Tully poked the extendable hand down to grab the ring, shifting aside scraps of flesh. As he leaned closer, he realised it weren't no ring. It was some kind of locket, dented and scraped by the grinder, but too stubborn to break and now wedged between two gears. Took a few goes before Tully could wiggle it out. He wiped off the blood, then raised it to the light, forcing the locket open. The squeaky hinges needed oiling. Inside the picture-frame was a faded photo of a girl, but that'd come out easily enough. The name engraved outside would be harder to remove, but he could fill that in with soldering wire.

Tully snapped the locket shut. Good silver. He started the grinder again to finish the giller off, smiling. That locket would fetch a decent price. *Madam Silk's* it was.

Chapter 24: Fireworks from Below

Kef stared up at the Lightning Tower. From where she was – a storage room in a neighbouring ship, just above water level – the Tower loomed tall and slender above her. Forks of lightning struck the spire high above. The Tower occupied Zorith's central point, standing tall in a clearing of calm water, with huge ships around it, all separated from the Tower by ninety feet of giller-patrolled sea. Chains ran from the surrounding boats to anchor the soaring structure.

In the glass-domed room at the Tower's peak, Exoran's arse-kissing contest had begun. Elsewhere in Zorith, other events were also about to begin – events that would get Kef inside the Tower.

Fireworks soared into the air, exploding into blue and white starbursts. They brightened Zorith's sky, crackling and fizzling. Throughout the city, people cheered.

"Zorith!" yelled one drunken man in the distance, starting a chant. "Zorith! Zorith!"

Hunched over in the storeroom, Kef gritted her teeth. Up in that glass-domed ballroom, Exoran's stupid honourborns were probably joining in with the cheers. Kef scowled. Of course they'd be cheering. But the rest of the city? Didn't those idiots realise the fireworks weren't for them?

A lightning bolt struck the spire above. Thunder boomed, drowning out the fireworks' crackle. The distant cheering dimmed a little. Kef grinned. Men and women played at making their own storms, but true storms could never be tamed.

She looked down from the porthole to check her equipment. Goggles, dangling around her neck. Alchemical globe cube in her pocket. Knives tucked in sheaths on either leg, and on her arms, and in the bandolier strapped across her chest. A spear gun was slung across her back, although hopefully she wouldn't need it, and her waterproof backpack held a blastpoint mine and four pistols with silencers attached, along with plenty of ammunition. In her vest, the pockets held Harold's all-important chemtabs, sealed inside waterproof ziplock bags, along with a few other mixtures. Everything she needed for distractions, poisonings, or explosions.

Kef felt a little anxious to be carrying the chemtabs, but Harold promised she'd be safe. His mixtures were two-part, he'd explained. They were inert until she peeled the tabs open, then stuck them onto their counterpart. All her tabs were in their own waterproof ziplock bags, and she kept each reactive set in different pockets on opposite sides of her body, just like Harold had recommended. He said that would be fine, but in Kef's experience, alchemy wasn't the most exact science. Still, she had to trust them. Stealing the Channeler depended on it.

Kef shook her head. She should stop calling it the Channeler, since she'd only been doing that in her head to stop herself accidently blurting the truth. No one else around to talk to now, though. All their plans were set. All the pieces were placed. Still, old habits were hard to kill.

She brushed her finger against the bracelet around her wrist. The bracelet was a promise, and tonight she'd make it come true.

A shrill squeaking echoed across the water. Kef looked through the porthole as a red flare hissed into Zorith's sky, ugly and stark amongst the blue and white fireworks. Kef's heartbeat quickened. That was the signal.

On the Lightning Tower's far side, water burst into the air. The shock wave shuddered through Kef's ship, rocking the floor beneath her. An alchemical mixture spread around the Lightning Tower's base, clouding the water and – if Harold had balanced it right – giving the gillers a mad fit of choking.

Kef opened her porthole. She put her goggles on, then lowered herself into the greasy water, moving slowly to avoid a splash. Oily chemicals slid over her skin, making her itch. She kept her eyes just above the water and clutched the porthole's rim to stop her diving weights from dragging her under. Near the Lightning Tower's base some ninety feet away, gillers burst through the surface, gasping. Kef smiled. Gills let them breathe underwater, but they also tended to absorb pollutants – and that included the chemicals dispersed by Harold's bomb.

Kef took a deep breath, filling her lungs to capacity. Then she dove underwater.

Zorith's cheering and the crackle of fireworks faded away. Now there was only quiet. Quietness, and a darkness thick enough to turn her hands into blurred smudges. She glided through the water. Squine was supposed to do this part. If he'd still been alive they wouldn't have needed the chemical cloud. Still, you had to play with the cards you had. And even down to her last card, Kef was a better player than most

Her diving weights pulled her down as she swam. She

focussed everything into the smooth movement of her hands, the regular kicking of her bare feet. No point in worrying about the gillers. Either they'd catch her, or Harold's chemicals would keep them away. Nothing she could do except focus on her next stroke. Strange, how waiting for action made her tense, but once she moved into motion, everything calmed.

A metal hull loomed before her. She bumped into the hull, grabbing onto ridges where the metal folded over each other. Gripping the hull, she pulled herself down. The darkness grew thicker. Once she'd dropped far enough, she shook a glow cube to activate its light. The pale blue light didn't dispel much of the gloom, but it was bright enough to show the depth markings on the hull. She was two-thirds of the way down that she needed to be.

Kef pulled herself deeper, tightness beginning to clamp against her lungs. She should still have plenty of air, though. Holding her glow cube above her wrist, she glanced at her waterproof timepiece. Forty seconds down. She'd managed three minutes of breath-holding in a contest, once. If everything went to plan, she'd be inside the Lightning Tower well before that.

The depth markings ticked by. Distant explosions thrummed through the water, pushing against her; those were Harold's bombs, which had taken most of the day to set up. The explosions created a slight pressure in Kef's ears, but she endured it knowing the pain would be ten times worse for any gillers who were still in the water, thanks to their enhanced senses. With every power came a weakness. Between the explosions and the alchemical slick, no giller would want to be diving down into the depths.

She reached the target marker, forty-five feet under the

waterline. Above her, the water grew brighter. Had they found some way to clear Harold's fog, or were her eyes simply adjusting to the gloom? She swam to the side, brushing her hand against the hull.

A hatch appeared. It was locked tight with no seams for her to pry open. Kef waited beside it, trying to ignore the tightening in her chest, telling herself that all the pain was in her mind. Her heartrate was low, the gillers hadn't found her, and she'd reached the intake hatch on schedule.

Kef glanced at her timepiece. Fifty-five seconds since Harold's red flare erupted into the sky. In five seconds, another bomb would disable Zorith's desalination plant. The shutdown would make the Lightning Tower switch to the backup system. Among the many things that activated, it would open this intake vent to draw water into the on-board desalination plant.

The pressure in Kef's lungs grew. She squeezed her eyes shut, wincing, then opened them to look at her timepiece. Sixty-five seconds had passed. The hatch was still closed. Kef frowned. She'd told Harold sixty seconds, clear as a knife.

So why was the hatch still shut?

She tapped it, then tried prising it apart, her fingers scrabbling against the metal. Pain stabbed through her eyes and ears. Her heartbeat accelerated. No, she had to stay calm and control her pulse, or she'd burn up too much oxygen.

Seventy seconds. The hatch was still shut. Kef slammed her fist against the metal, feeling the dull thump run up her arm. Had Harold betrayed her? Had he always been planning to give hope, only to rip it away? The bastard!

Kef prepared to ascend. She had to go now, or she'd lose her window to reach the surface before blacking out. Once she broke through, the gillers would see her, but she could take them, she had the spear gun and her knives –

The hatch slid open. Bubbles flumed up to the surface and water rushed into the pipe behind the hatch, yanking Kef forward, slamming her into a grate stretched across the opening. Kef cursed, struggling against the water's pressure. Gabine hadn't mentioned a grate. The bastards must've installed it themselves.

Kef drew a knife to stab the grate, still struggling to overcome the water's pressure. Her blow made the grate flex, but it held. Damn. She needed something stronger.

Her lungs strained. She got her feet onto the grate, then pushed herself up, standing sideways on the metal, stuck to it by the force of the rushing water. Reaching into her vest, she pulled out a pair of Harold's chemtabs, marked with three green lines. She peeled off the wrappings, slammed the two halves together, dropped them into the current and dove to the side. The tab slapped into the grate. Kef dragged herself away from the vent, clawing at any holds she could find. Harold said she'd have five seconds from the moment of combining the mixtures, but five seconds was hard to count when her heartbeat was thumping hot in her ears and water was trying to drag her away.

A shockwave slammed into Kef and the explosion's muffled thump clapped against her ears. The force shoved her sideways, making her spin in the water. Her knife twisted away, along with her glow cube, sinking into the dark. Blackness engulfed her. She thrust a panicked hand out and somehow caught a handhold.

Gritting her teeth, she dragged herself back towards the grate. Or at least where she hoped the grate was, because without her glow cube she was blinded by the inky gloom. Damn it, this was annoying. She even had one of Harold's serums tucked in her pocket – a serum that would enhance her night vision – but if she took that now, she'd be blinded by the light when she got into the Tower, because the stupid thing took an hour to wear off.

Ringing echoed in her ears. That explosion better have blasted a hole in the grate. Better not have caught the giller's attention, either. Hopefully, all the other underwater bombs would distract them. Hopefully, the chemical slick was too toxic for them to bear. Hopefully, she would find this grate because her lungs ached and even if Kef ascended she couldn't reach the surface in time and her ears felt ready to burst and all she felt was smooth unbroken hull –

Her shin cracked against a sharp corner. She winced, wanting to curse. Wait. A sharp corner ...

She reached out with her boot and felt it pass beyond where the hull should be. Twisting around, she fumbled into the darkness. The grate pressed against her fingers, mangled and buckled from the explosion. Inching her hand up, she felt a hole gaping in the middle.

Kef dragged herself through. Her limbs scraped against the metal as she squeezed through the intake pipe. Gabine said it was big enough for maintenance workers to crawl through, but it felt tight for Kef. Her head pounded. How long had she been under? Two minutes? Three? Coldness pierced her chest. This would be her grave. After all the hardship she'd endured, all the battles she'd fought, all the crooks she'd swindled and friends who'd betrayed her, this was how it ended?

No. If she was anyone else she would have died a hundred times before now. But she hadn't, because she *wasn't* anyone

197

else. She was Kef Cutmark, and just like all those other certain deaths she'd dragged herself away from, she'd drag herself out of this one, too.

Strength flooded back into her muscles. She kept wriggling forward through the black water, curling her body around the first bend. Another corner and then she'd be near the exit. More dragging, more crawling, light-headedness making her woozy, more wriggling, more squirming, then she was around the second bend and her head crashed into the first filter and her hands fumbled at the hatch built into the pipe's side, gripping the wheel, yanking on it with all the strength her fading muscles could muster and it wasn't going to turn and fuck this was her death wasn't it except she somehow dug deeper and tugged on the wheel harder and it groaned clockwise and frantic joy swooped through her and she kept spinning the wheel and then the hatch swung open and she crawled in, the pressure crushing around her and all her senses fading and a voice like a scream bouncing around her skull, death calling for her, but death had to wait because with the last of her strength Kef dragged herself up around another bend –

And her head broke through the water's surface.

She gasped. Water gushed from her coughing mouth. She slipped under the surface, flailing hands splashing the water, but then she wedged her feet against either side of the pipe to force herself up into that blessed air. Blessed, sweet air. Sweeter than anything she'd ever tasted.

She stayed there, inhaling giant lungfuls of air. Her hands shook. Darkness surrounded her, her ears were still ringing from the explosion, and her heart pounded. But she was alive. And she'd done it!

Kef raised her hand into the air in a weak celebration. Her knuckles crashed into metal above her. She cursed, wincing. No time to celebrate. Getting into the Lightning Tower was supposed to be the easy bit, but it had almost killed her. That didn't bode well for the struggles ahead.

She slipped her spear gun off from her shoulders and let it sink down below. Wouldn't be useful for close-quarters fighting inside the Tower, and it would just get in the way. She reached up to grab the hatch. A strong twist had the wheel squeaking, then a few more turns made a mechanism click. A sliver of light knifed into the pipe as she opened the hatch. She winced as she did it, half expecting the water to come flooding up from under her now that there was no pressure seal above, especially since she was still a good forty feet under water level, but Gabine had designed this pipe well.

Bright light made Kef squint as she opened the hatch all the way. Taking a deep breath, she clambered out into the Engine Room.

Chapter 25: It Stares Back Also

Kef emerged in a room full of hissing tubes, strange machinery, and mazelike walkways twisting over each other. The walkways rattled from the rumbling generator. As she straightened up, a blast of heat smacked into her.

"Don't touch any orange pipes," she remembered Gabine saying. *"Orange means the contents are running at boiling point."*

Judging by the distant clanking of boots, several workers occupied the engine room. Sneaking past them wouldn't be too difficult – no screeching klaxons meant her entrance hadn't triggered any alarms. Still, she had to be careful. If one person found her too early, all her plans would collapse.

Kef closed the hatch, then snuck off to a hidden corner behind a tangle of pipes. She opened her waterproof backpack, dried herself with the microfiber towel, slipped her feet into boots, holstered her guns, checked the other supplies, then zipped the bag back up.

The engine room was a labyrinth of walkways, equipment, and ladders. Even with her good memory and Gabine's drawings, it took Kef a while to orient herself. Fortunately, the jumble of pipes made it easy to sneak through the room. Her soft-soled boots made only the faintest taps as she climbed ladders and crept around workers. The machinery's noisy rumbling masked any slight noises Kef made.

Kef reached the engine room's top level. She sighed. Truth be told, she'd almost wished someone would spot her. Then all this pent-up anxiety she had about getting caught could explode out into a brawl. Plank always said the best battle was one you didn't have to fight, but Kef had never quite adopted that way of thinking.

She slipped out of the engine room and stepped into stairwell 2E's bottom level, easing the door shut behind her. When her boot landed on the first step, it made a strange squeak. Kef frowned. No, that didn't sound like the steps had made it. It sounded like something else had. She backed down, drew her knife, then walked around to peer under the steps.

Hiding under the stairs, a little girl stared back. Her hand pressed over her mouth as she tried to muffle her giggles. Kef froze. If that girl was a guard, Kef would've buried her knife in her throat and clamped her hand across her lips to silence the girl's dying screams, but this girl looked no older than seven. That made Kef pause. And with her pause came weakness. If the girl wanted to yell, she'd be able to do it before Kef could silence her.

"Shh!" said the girl. "I'm hiding."

She sounded rather proud of that fact, considering how easy Kef found her. Kef frowned. Something about that voice, that face …

"Who are you hiding from?" Kef whispered, trying to buy time.

"The guards." The girl flashed Kef a smug grin. "They're meant to be baby-sitting me, but I snuck away and now they can't find me."

Kef forced herself to smile. She didn't know the first thing about kids, but whenever adults wanted them to do something they always seemed to smile. Smile or shout, those seemed the two options. Only one was available, for obvious reasons.

"I won't bother you, then," Kef said. "In fact, I'm hiding, too, so let's keep our lips shut and not tell anyone else about this."

The girl pouted. "You can't be hiding as well! Only I can be hiding."

"Well ... I'm playing a different game, then."

"No you can't! There's only one game and only one hider, and that's me, and you have to do what I want because my Daddy's the High Captain."

Kef froze. "Your father ... is Exoran?"

Triumph gleamed in her eyes. "That's right, so there."

Kef's stomach clenched. Made sense that Exoran's daughter would be just as much of a cruel bastard as him. Still holding her knife behind her back, Kef adjusted her grip. Blood thumped through her skull. She'd been planning on leaving this kid alive. But now ...

"Okay, I'm sorry." Kef inched closer to the girl, still keeping her knife behind her back. "I'll stop hiding, then."

The girl's smug little smile grew broader. Kef's face twitched. That was Exoran's smile. The one he'd worn when she'd pleaded for him to stop, and when she'd begged for release. Kef swallowed. Exoran had taken everything from her. Her family. Her dignity. Her childhood. And now his arrogant little princess of a girl crouched under the stairs, hiding. Pretending that avoiding guards was a fun game. Not the difference between whether you survived to keep scraping food and water from the streets – or whether they beat you to death and laughed while they did it. She might only be a child, but

202

Kef could already see a streak of viciousness dripping from the girl, dark as Exoran's. Killing this girl wouldn't be a crime. It would be a mercy to the world. It would be the justice Kef deserved.

She stepped towards the girl, watching with satisfaction as her cocky little smile faded. Kef made her choice.

Chapter 26: Fireworks from Above

In the glass-domed ballroom, High Captain Exoran watched fireworks explode into the night sky, hands clasped behind his back. Fawning honourborns applauded and cheered. Personally, Exoran didn't see the appeal. Still, he was trying to show his power to the honourborns, and these silly fizzlers signified that.

Exoran sighed. Things were simpler when he'd been the Lightning Tower's Overseer. He'd never imagined returning to the Tower like this. His gaze swept around the room as music began to play. When he'd been Overseer, this glass-domed area held their desks. Now the spot where his desk used to be was occupied by a miniature model of Zorith, with the boats and walkways moulded from edible resin in exquisite detail. In the centre of the display, the Lightning Tower matched Exoran's considerable height. Chocolate flowed down the miniature tower to fill the waterways running through the city.

Back when this ballroom was an office, hundreds of administrators, engineers, and clerks filled this room. The workspace was so hot that in the afternoon they would hand out salt pills. Clearly, the original designers never expected the Tower to require so many workers. These days, Exoran knew better. Build an empire and you needed another two just to administrate the thing.

Now, honourborns crowded the room. On the edges, people chatted, laughed, and nibbled on canapes. In the middle, partners danced with formal grace. You wouldn't have thought they were all waiting anxiously for Exoran to announce his new governors. Although perhaps they were trying to act more relaxed than normal – an exaggerated peal of laughter here, an overloud voice there. Sometimes he caught a group watching him over their drinks. They glanced away the instant he spotted them. Good. Keeping these sort of people nervous was one of the few pleasures remaining to him.

Lightning struck the Tower's spire. The bolt streaked down the metal, coursing through a pole that joined the dome's apex to the floor below. Blue light glowed from the lightning rod, filtered through layers of insulative glass wrapped around the pole. It was bright enough to illuminate the room, but too dim to make these soft-eyed honourborns wince. The sound was muted, too; the thunder was barely audible compared to the music, even though the lightning had directly struck the Tower.

"High Captain Exoran."

Exoran didn't recognise that voice. He turned to see a thin, diminutive man wearing a red tuxedo and a crooked grin. A black rose protruded from his breast pocket, wreathed in small, thorny tendrils. A small hourglass dangled from a thin rope around his neck; inside, sand flowed down into the bottom chamber. Before the top could empty, the falling sand swapped direction, rising back into the upper section. Exoran blinked. It must have been some kind of alchemical trick

Exoran's guards stood beside the man. He didn't recognise

205

this guest – and he knew every honourborn in Zorith – but he nodded to the guards, who let the man step forward.

"Who are you?" Exoran asked.

"I have more names than you have time. We'll go with the one I'm most often called." The man's lips twitched. "Well, maybe not that one, because it's not particularly pleasant to refined ears. The next, then: Daen."

Exoran's frown deepened. He couldn't place the name's origin, or that accent, either.

"I don't recall your name on the guest list, Daen."

"You wrote that yourself, did you? I would've thought a man of your demands would be far too busy for such trifles."

"I like control."

Daen's crooked smile widened. "Don't we all?"

With a grand sweep of his hand, somehow keeping his champagne glass from spilling over, Daen gestured to the exploding fireworks, which illuminated the crests of nearby waves.

"The Twisted Seas! Last refuge of humanity! Friend to sailors! Scourge of sailors! Monsters and treasures and pirates and glory and tempests and clear skies! Chaos incarnate, and we are specks not even worthy to be tormented by its capricious storms." Daen sipped his champagne. "Mostly, at least."

Exoran sighed. He didn't know how this drunkard had snuck inside his event, but he wanted him gone.

"For one claiming to know how busy I am," he said. "You seem set on wasting my time. Guards, take him away."

Exoran's bodyguards strode towards Daen. Really, he could've probably ordered a single guard to escort the man away. One of his bodyguards would weigh twice as much as the diminutive man.

"Ah ha, I wouldn't do that!" Daen raised his hands, keeping his champagne glass balanced between his fingers. "Unless you want to miss a deal you sorely need."

The bodyguards paused an arm span away from Daen.

Exoran scowled. "I didn't tell you to stop."

Shrugging, the bodyguards grabbed Daen. Except – somehow – Daen slipped through their grip to step up close to Exoran, his champagne glass still carefully balanced, unspilled and unsipped in his hand.

"It's about what's really in the Channeler," Daen whispered.

The guards grabbed Daen, pulling him away. Coldness pierced Exoran's chest. Around him, partygoers turned to look at the commotion.

"No, leave him," said Exoran. "I want to talk."

The bodyguards released Daen, scowling at him. He smiled, raising his champagne glass. Despite being wrestled backwards, it was still full to the brim.

Exoran pointed to an empty section of the ballroom, right at the centre. There was a clearing around the lightning rod. It seemed that no guests wanted to stand within twenty feet of it, even though the device was perfectly safe.

"Come," he said.

He strode through the party, his mind racing. Daen waltzed beside him, humming in tune with the music. Exoran stroked his chin. Daen was bluffing, because how could he know about what was in the Tower?

Exoran stopped beside the lightning rod, encased within thick layers of glass. Another bolt struck the spire high above, making the rod glow.

"Most impressive." Daen gazed at the flickering light. "Do

207

you mind if I touch it?"

"Knock yourself out."

"Oh no, it looks quite well insulated."

Daen stroked the glass. A hungry look flashed in his eyes.

"You mentioned you had a deal," said Exoran.

"Ah, yes, the deal." Daen pointed at the ground. "I want one of them."

"One of what?"

"You know what I'm discussing." Daen's eyes twinkled. "Unless you want me to say it aloud …"

Exoran glanced over his shoulder. Guilty-looking honour-borns turned away, coughing into their drinks.

"No, I understand."

"I thought you would. You seem like a clever boy."

Exoran snorted. "Boy? You look like you've barely escaped childhood."

"Why, thank you. I've aged well, all things considered. Now, our deal." Daen pressed his hands together. "I want one."

"And in return?"

"Why, the whole world, my friend!"

"I'll need something more tangible than that."

Daen blinked. "I scarcely think there is anything more tangible. Or more valuable. When a man has but one option, he'd do well not to lose it."

"Look, tell me what you're offering and we can negotiate."

"But I have, dear Exoran."

"You're not getting one for free."

Daen smiled. "Nothing in life comes for free. Nothing in death, either."

"Then my answer shouldn't surprise you."

"Surprised? No." Daen glanced at his timepiece and Exoran

frowned at the strange symbols and dials etched into the clockface. "Disappointed? Very. You've made me lose my bet. Oh well, not to worry. I'll have what I want soon enough, one way or another."

Daen's eyes shifted away from Exoran, looking over his shoulder. "Hmm. I thought Zorith's colours were blue and white."

Frowning, Exoran glanced behind him. A red flare soared into the sky, crackling and sparking, standing out amidst the blue and white fireworks. Around the ballroom, people gasped and the music grew fragmented before the conductor reasserted control. Exoran scowled. Those rioters were at it again. He would send guards to find the flare's launcher. Zorith needed order. Control. There was no more room for dissent, not with the threats looming large on the horizon.

Exoran turned back to Daen.

The man was gone.

Exoran blinked. He'd looked away for only a few moments. How was this possible?

He beckoned to one of his bodyguards. "Tom, did you see Daen disappear?"

Tom shook his head. "Sorry, sir. I was looking at that flare."

"Weren't we all," muttered Exoran. "Tell the other guards to find Daen."

"Very good. May our ships float forever, sir."

"Yes. May our ships float forever."

Tom strode into the crowd. Exoran sighed. He didn't know what Daen had been plotting, but he knew one thing for sure: his guards wouldn't find that man tonight.

Chapter 27: Inside the Heart

Kef snuck along the curving hallway, keeping herself pressed to the inner wall. With each bang of fireworks, light flashed through the portholes on her right side, making shadows shift and dance. Less frequent were the sharp booms of lightning and thunder – but when they came, they flared through the corridor, bright as daylight.

Footsteps echoed from around the bend. Wincing, Kef doubled her pace, creeping forward. She pressed herself up against a door, trying to stay calm, then took her picks out from her pocket. She went to work on the lock. The footsteps grew closer.

The lock clicked. As a shadow stretched around the corridor's bend, she opened the door to slip inside, easing it shut behind her.

The broom closet reeked of ammonia. Kef unsheathed her knife, pressing her ear against the wooden door. Outside, the footsteps grew closer, closer, closer … then faded away. She breathed out a relieved sigh. Sneaking up through the Lightning Tower had been a tricky affair. If it weren't for Gabine's plans, she'd never have made it. Creeping around the corridors had reminded Kef of when she'd been here before, and those were memories she didn't want to relive.

Faint light shone under the door from the corridor. Kef opened one of Harold's chemtabs, smearing the green paste into a circle on the metal floor. She peeled open another tab, then daubed its contents onto the smeared paste. A hiss filled the air.

Kef wrapped a mask over her mouth and nose to block the noxious fumes rising from the acid. She stood, unsheathing knives to hold a blade in either hand. The circle on the floor glowed red as the acid ate through the metal, just like Harold's chemicals had done in the Alchemical Factory.

Kef stomped on the weakened floor. Her boot crunched against the circle of damaged metal, knocking a disc clear to clatter into the room below. Kef dropped through the hole.

She landed in a windowless room, surrounded by four guards. Springing up, she hurled her knife at the one nearest the emergency lever. The blade stabbed through his neck, pinning him against the wall. Her next throwing-knife sunk into another guard's shoulder, making him collapse.

Cursing, the other two guards struggled to free their own knives. She pounced on the nearest before he reached his weapon, sliding around, wrapping her hand across his face, then twisting his neck until it snapped. The other guard lunged at her with his dagger. She pivoted to shove the dead man onto his blade, wrenching it from his grip. As he stumbled, she drew another knife and sliced across his jugular.

He dropped onto the floor. Blood spurted from his neck, and when he tried to stop the flow with his hands, it sprayed between his fingers, splattering across the ceiling. He opened his mouth to scream. Before he could, Kef rammed her knife through his eye socket. His hands flopped away from his neck.

Kef hunched over, panting. Four guards down in four

211

seconds. Too bad no one was keeping score.

A pitiful moan came from her left, followed by a dragging scrape. Kef whirled around, drawing another knife. On the floor, one of the guards she'd taken down had crawled to the wall, the point of Kef's throwing knife sticking up through a shoulder matted with blood. He reached up for the emergency lever with a trembling hand.

"No!" Kef said.

She hurled her knife, aiming for his hand, but her spinning blade barely nicked his finger, burying itself into the wall. With a triumphant snarl, the man yanked the lever.

Her next throw speared into the back of his neck, turning that snarl into a strangled gurgle. He slumped to the ground.

Red lights flashed through the room and a klaxon shrieked. Kef cursed. With his last breath, the guard had activated the alarm, alerting security to lock down the base. She dashed over to the key rack, grabbing the ones she needed. There were hundreds of keys in this room, but she knew which one to pick. Even after fifteen years, she remembered exactly what they looked like, the same way she remembered Exoran's every smirk, every blow, every scar he'd carved onto her flesh. She thought again of his daughter. Had she made the right choice?

Kef sprinted out of the room. No time left to grab her knives. Luckily, she still had plenty tucked in her bandolier. As she dashed along the corridor, she unholstered her guns, knowing that there was no more use for stealth, not with klaxons screeching and red lights flashing.

She kicked in the door to the stairwell, then powered up the steps. Despite her pounding heartbeat, a cold clarity made her surroundings sharp and dampened her aches. Years and years, and now she was back. And close, so close it hurt to think about, but she had to stay focussed.

Above her, a door slammed open. Two guards strode onto the landing, gaping down at her. They tried to grab their guns, but before their revolvers could clear their holsters, Kef raised her two pistols and shot. Bullets burst through their skulls, splattering blood across the wall. She was out the door before their corpses hit the ground.

As she slid out into the corridor, the klaxon's wailing stopped, but the flashing red lights continued. Exoran probably didn't want to alarm his guests. Well, that would be the least of his worries in a few minutes.

She reached a large steel door. It was plain, with no markings to give away what was inside, but she knew what it contained right away. She opened it with the stolen key, slipped into the short corridor, then locked it behind her.

Another door lay ahead. Unlike the outer door she'd passed through, this one was circular and sturdy, resembling the entrance to a bank vault, and made from an alchemical resin Gabine claimed was stronger than steel. A large wheel stuck out from the middle of the door, right next to the keyhole. Above the wheel, a peephole looked into the room beyond, covered by a rubber flap. A red-lettered sign held bolded words:

Channeler Room, primary entrance. WARNING: high voltage, extreme danger. Before entering, wear appropriate protective gear, remove any metal, and ensure rear airlock door is closed. Follow procedure 45-B. May our ships float forever.

A bulky locker lined one side of the short hallway. Kef opened it to reveal full-body plastic containment suits – the kind alchemists used when dealing with dangerous experiments. She slashed the suits with her knife. There were

213

probably other suits somewhere else, but this would slow them down.

She pulled a blastpoint mine from her backpack, then placed it on the floor, pointing at the outer door that led into the main corridor. Moving fast, she uncurled the tripwire lines, placing the trigger pads around the entrance. When guards stormed inside, they would be greeted with a painful surprise.

There. That was all her preparations done. She wouldn't have needed them if the alarm had stayed silent, but thankfully she'd planned for the worst.

She strode towards the inner vault door, then took a deep breath. How odd to be on this side. Fifteen years, and she was back …

Someone slammed into the outer door behind her, making Kef flinch.

"She must be inside!" yelled a guard in the corridor. "Get the backup keys, go!"

Footsteps raced away. Kef gritted her teeth. No time for delaying. Yet now that she was here, she didn't want to go inside. But she had to, even if her hand was shaking as she gripped the wheel, even if she knew her chances of escaping were dwindling with every second she spent here.

Using the stolen key, she unlocked the door, then spun the wheel to ease it open a few inches. She twisted her grip to break the key, leaving a remnant inside the lock. She still had another copy of the key, which she would use to lock the door after entering.

Kef opened the door all the way. Then – after taking a deep breath – she strode inside.

Chapter 28: Can't Take it from You

S oft green grass met Kef's boots as she walked into the room, locking the vault door behind her. Inside, water trickled from a hidden fountain and plants covered the walls, obscuring the metal she knew lay behind the foliage. There were no windows, but yellow ceiling lamps glowed with the impression of daylight. A pleasant citrus scent filled the room. Something furry rubbed against Kef's leg and she looked down to see a shaggy puppy gazing up at her with adoring eyes.

She gaped. This was wrong. What had happened?

Kef looked back up, trying to focus. In the middle of the circular room, a lightning rod hung from the ceiling, ending in a metal ball three feet above the floor. Four men and three women stood around the conducting ball. They wore sleeveless grey smocks made from a strange shimmering material. Identical tattoos bearing Zorith's emblem covered the backs of their left hands. They stared at Kef.

"Katie?" a hunchbacked old man shuffled towards Kef. "Is that you?"

His voice was whispery and thin, like tissue paper crumpling. But underneath that frailty was warmth, and concern, and love.

Kef raced forward, wrapping her arms around the old man, pulling him into a hug.

"It's me." She sniffed. "My name's Kef, now, but … it's me, Samu."

She wanted to say more. So much more. But a ball of phlegm formed in her mouth, constricting her throat, and her vision blurred. Kef pressed her eyes shut and squeezed him tighter. A slight gasp came out of him, warm breath rushing over her ear, and she realised how lean and delicate he'd become. His ribs pushed up against her chest and she felt them straining under the pressure of her hug. Swallowing, she released him.

She barely had a second to recover before Eliza jumped onto her. Kef hugged her back. She laughed. Was this how Samu felt when Kef had wrapped him in a crushing hug? Either way, she liked it. Growing up in this wretched prison, Eliza had been the one light in the darkness. Back then, they'd both been little girls. Even though Eliza was now a head taller than Kef, the hug felt so familiar that it was like they'd seen each other yesterday.

She closed her eyes, savouring the feeling of Eliza's warm ear pressed against her cheek. Eliza had given Kef the strength to escape. And she'd given her the courage to return. Kef stroked her thumb against the rope-bracelet around her wrist. That was Eliza's gift, the night before her escape. A painful gift, at times, anchoring her to a past she'd rather forget, but all the weight and agony of that anchor had been worth it for this reunion.

"You smell different," Eliza whispered.

Kef opened her eyes and reality rushed back to greet her. She released Eliza. Wrenching her gaze away, Kef pinched her thigh, trying to focus.

216

The other Lightning Callers stared at her. A smile creased Ann's wrinkled face as she stretched an arm around Samu, who was wiping tears from his eyes. Thamar, Elliot, and Flora all smiled, like they couldn't comprehend Kef's presence.

The only one frowning was Yew. He placed his hand on the conducting ball, summoning a bolt of energy that raced down the lightning rod. Electricity crackled through his body. With his other hand he touched a pole that stuck out of the ground, making the energy flow into the pole, disappearing through the ground to the batteries below. Kef shook her head. A lot had changed since she'd last been here, but Yew's surly dedication had stayed constant.

This was Zorith's secret. A machine didn't power the Lightning Tower. It was powered by slaves. Lightning Callers: blessed or bred or cursed by who knew what to summon electricity from the skies. When she was four, Kef had been taken to the Tower. For a decade after that, these men and women had been her fellow prisoners – until she'd escaped, fifteen years ago.

"Katie." Samu rolled that word around, savouring it. "Why are you here?"

Kef adjusted position so that Eliza had a better view of her face. The girl was deaf, but she could read Kef's lips just fine.

"When I left, I made a promise." She swallowed, trying to stop her voice from shaking. "Today I keep it."

A loud bang came from the entrance. Kef whirled around. Bootsteps clattered into the airlock outside –

Her blastpoint mine exploded. Guards screamed and cursed and the floor trembled.

"It's trapped, get back, get back!" yelled someone.

"Katie, what's happening?" asked Samu, shrinking away

217

from her.

A body slammed against the other side of the inner door. "She's there!"

Kef strode towards the door, drawing a weapon from her bag.

"I can see her!" said the guard outside. "In the peephole –"

Kef stabbed a stiletto knife through the peephole, shattering the glass to drive the blade into the guard's eye. He squealed, stumbling back from the door. A click sounded as another guard slid a key inside the lock, but judging by the dull thud, Kef's broken key had blocked theirs.

Kef slapped the door. "I've got guns, you fuckers! First person in here gets a bullet to the brain."

The key's jiggling stopped. Kef nodded. The threats and the jammed lock wouldn't hold them forever, but hopefully it would give her a few minutes.

She turned back to the seven Lightning Callers. Eliza put her hand to her mouth, and the others backed away from Kef, gaping.

All except for Yew, who just raised an eyebrow. "You've changed, girl."

"And you got old," said Kef.

She dropped her backpack on the ground, pulling out a chemtab marked with a lightning bolt. Unlike the other chemtabs, these had more weight to it, as requested. She peeled the two halves apart, then threw it at a patch of ceiling that was clear of vines. The sticky sides glued themselves to the metal.

"What are you doing?" asked Samu.

"I'm here to free you."

Yew rolled his eyes. The others looked even more shocked,

which annoyed Kef. Surely, when someone burst into your prison, it should be clear what they were planning to do. She gave them slack, though. Seeing her alive after fifteen years would be rather surprising.

"How?" Yew stepped away from the conductor ball. "There's only one route out of here and it's filled with guards."

"No. There's another way. There always is."

"What is it, then?"

"Can't tell you. Those guards are listening to everything I say. Just follow my lead."

Kef grabbed a long wire from her backpack, with magnets at either end. She threw one end against the chemtab stuck to the ceiling. The magnet hit the chemtab with a clank, fixing itself in place.

"What is she doing?" a guard muttered from behind the door.

"Quiet!" said another.

Kef tucked the wire's other end under her armpit, then strode towards the conductor ball, letting the wire spool out behind her. As she walked, she fidgeted with her hands. Eliza's eyes widened. She nudged Ann, who nodded and placed a finger on her lips. The other Callers watched Kef intently.

Heavy bootsteps clunked in the corridor outside. Kef swallowed. More guards.

When she reached the conductor ball, she slapped the wire's other end onto the metal. The magnet clanked against the ball.

"Wait." Yew frowned at the wire joining the conductor ball to the chemtab on the ceiling. "You haven't asked if we want to be free."

Kef frowned. "What?"

Yew gestured at the lush plants sprawling around the room,

at the vines covering the metal walls, at the puppy who'd been cowering behind a fern ever since Kef stabbed the guard through the peephole.

"It's not like when you were here," Yew said.

Kef winced. She'd done her best to forget the tortures endured in this room, but she'd never been able to stop them crawling into her mind. Whips, lacerating skin. Hair, ripped from her head. Knives, slashed across her arms. Guards laughing and placing wagers to see who'd be the first to beg for mercy. And, above it all, the Tower's Overseer. Exoran. Back then she hadn't known his name. But she'd known his face, and his orders, and his cold cruelty, and she'd hated him with every fiery inch of her body.

"After you escaped, they punished us," said Yew. "But once they realised that we didn't know where you'd gone, they stopped. They weaned us off Zetamyre and brought all these plants and luxuries. Ever since you've gone, it's been nice. We can never leave this room, of course, but as far as prisons go, it's a good one. Better than the chaos that's out there. I remember what it was like to live on the seas. Violence. Fear. Always squabbling for something another person has. Here, they feed us three times a day, and it's good. Fit for honourborns! They bring in whatever books we want. Plants, as well. Even pets, like Wap." Yew pointed to the puppy, who barked, sounding uncertain. "You don't have to free us, Kef. We like this."

Kef shook her head. "No. No, you can't mean this. You don't know what I've sacrificed!"

She turned to plead with the others. They all looked away from her, guilt etched across their faces. In the corridor outside, the guards laughed.

"Stupid bitch, they don't want you!" shouted a guard.

220

"Samu?" Kef grabbed the old man's wrinkled hand. "Tell me you don't want this. Please!"

He bowed his head.

"I'm sorry, Katie," he said in his warm, whispery voice.

"No." Tears streaked down Kef's sweat-stained face. "No!"

She yanked Samu towards the conductor ball, then slapped his hand onto the metal. Her fingers brushed the metal, alongside his. The ball rumbled. She wrenched herself backwards, pulling Samu away. Lightning shot down the rod, striking the ball and sending energy crackling through the wire she'd attached to the chemtab on the ceiling.

The chemtab exploded.

Light blinded Kef and a shockwave hurled her backwards. Grass and dirt sprayed into her mouth. She bit her tongue and tasted blood as she rolled to a stop.

Groaning, she forced her eyes open, trying to ignore the shrill ringing in her ears. The room was dark. She'd short-circuited the lights.

A faint brightness came from the scorched metal edges of the hole cut through the ceiling by the chemtab. Through the hole, she saw shadowy glimpses of the glass-domed room above, where well-dressed honourborns stumbled and fell, made into murky outlines against the night sky.

Around Kef, Lightning Callers sprawled on the ground, tangled in their grey smocks. More people laid amongst them – honourborns who'd fallen from the room above, knocked unconscious from the drop. Everyone was a shadowy blur.

Kef staggered towards Samu. Or at least where she thought the old man was. Gabine said this room's insulative coating and faraday cage would stop lightning from destroying the walls, but combined with Harold's directional explosive, Kef had found a way through. She just wished it hadn't been so noisy. Her ears still throbbed and the Lightning Callers were still laying on the ground.

She shook Samu's body. "Samu! Are you alright?"

Her voice sounded strange, like someone had stuffed wool in her ears. Samu's frail hand clutched Kef's bicep. She helped him stand.

"Take this." She pressed a gun into his hand. "I'll get the others."

She staggered around as fast as she could manage, checking the Lightning Callers were okay. A few times she stumbled over fallen honourborns by accident – one man who'd remained conscious clutched her leg, so she knocked him out with a kick to the head.

"Come on, Callers," she yelled. "Get up, the seven of you!"

The ringing in her ears faded a little. In the glass-domed ballroom, people screamed and boots clattered as honourborns raced for the exits. Chaos. Kef smiled. Just as she'd planned.

Light flared from the entrance door. Kef glanced behind her to see the metal glowing. They must have found an oxyacetylene torch. The door was strong, but even the toughest metal could have a hole cut through it, as she'd so aptly demonstrated.

"Away from the exits!" yelled someone in the room above. "No one's leaving!"

Kef froze. That was Exoran's voice. To think he was so near, and that she was so close to her vengeance ... no, she had to stick to the plan, or everything would be lost.

One of the Lightning Callers was still on the ground. Eliza. Kef dragged her up, and pulled her over to Samu, who grasped her hand. Eliza had been deaf from birth, and while she could read lips and understand sign language, neither of those worked in the almost total darkness. She must have been scared out of her mind. Kef hated to put her through this, but it was the only way.

Sparks flew from a glowing finger-sized hole in the entrance door. A few more minutes and they'd cut through the lock.

"Take these," Kef said, giving guns to the Lightning Callers, then handing her backpack to Samu. "Careful, the safeties are off. Now, follow me!"

Something crashed into her temple, knocking her to the floor, thumping her head into the grass. Wooziness flooded through Kef. Wincing, she tried to stand, but she only managed to roll onto her back.

She glanced up, pain lancing through her skull. Yew stood over her. Lightning crackled between his fingers, illuminating his face, the other Callers, and the rest of the room.

"What?" she croaked, squinting from the light.

"We're sorry," said Yew. "But I told you before. We don't want freedom."

"No!" The word was a mumbled gasp, distorted by the spittle foaming from her mouth. "It's there. We can be free!"

Guards laughed behind the door. They hadn't burned through yet, but now it didn't matter. She would fail without them even lifting a finger. Everything blurred in and out of focus. The seven Lightning Callers looked down at her, guilt and shame spread across their faces, and the dizziness spinning through Kef's head made her want to puke.

Her hands twitched as she tried to reach up towards Yew. Scowling, Yew wrenched her hands aside. He swung the gun at her head and everything exploded in a shower of light.

Chapter 29: Evening Obligations

Nicholas had a problem.

He raised his glass to his mouth, letting the wine touch his lips, but not pass any further. Over the rim, he stared at High Captain Exoran. A gaggle of fawning honourborns clustered around the man, laughing at every word he uttered, and shouting over each other to talk to him. With a huff, Nicholas lowered his glass.

His problem was that everyone else had copied his idea. And, unlike him, they were succeeding. Imitation. Such is the curse of genius. Still, there was at least an hour until the High Captain announced his new governing council. Plenty of time for Nicholas to pull him aside for a few minutes, then tell Exoran how well Nicholas had been performing as his spy. He just had to get an audience with him.

Nicholas looked around the ballroom. Fireworks filled the night sky above Zorith – blue and white, as was proper, unlike that ghastly red flare some rabble had set off earlier. Nicholas would never permit such chaos if he was in charge.

A huge thunderclap of noise smashed into him and a bright flash stabbed into his eyes. Blackness clouded his vision. When he opened his eyes, he was lying on the ground without any memory of falling, his drink spilled all over his gorgeous jacket and the room around him dark and filled with a ringing echo.

Nicholas propped himself up with his elbows, whimpering. Dust and wine covered his face. His head hurt. What had happened?

Smoke rose from the other side of the room. Amongst the scattered bodies, barely visible in the darkness, a hole had punched through the ballroom's floor. The edges glowed with red light. Apart from that light, the room was dark. A hole … in the floor … and a thunderous noise … an explosion.

Exactly as K had foretold.

He reached into his pocket, pulling out the hip-flask K had given him. Thinking back to that rain-lashed night, he shuddered. When she'd dangled him from the clock-tower, he thought he was going to die. It had made him question many things. For all his proclamations about his political skills, how far had he come, really? Further than most men his age, especially men who had started low on society's ladder, but not as high as he could have. Certainly not as far as he would have liked. As he'd stumbled away from the clock tower, he had become more determined than ever. No longer would he content himself with sleep-ins and lazy mornings. Maybe he wasn't the most handsome, or the wealthiest, but he would make up for it by being the hardest working, and the bravest, and the smartest. And tonight was his chance to prove it.

Nicholas drank from the hipflask. He gagged. The serum tasted like dishwater. Or at least what he imagined dishwater would taste like, since he was above such menial chores.

The room grew light enough for him to read a fallen menu. When K said this serum would grant him night vision, he'd been doubtful, but the effect was truly incredible. It went to

225

show how well-resourced the High Captain's spies were. Soon Nicholas would have those resources for himself, but only if he proved his worth to K.

Around Nicholas, honourborns picked themselves up, groaning. Nicholas stood along with them. As per K's instructions, he'd stayed on the sternwards side of the ballroom, which meant he had been relatively far from the explosion. Those nearer to the hole hadn't fared well. Some had fallen in. Others lay on the floor, unmoving.

"A bomb," someone muttered in a groggy voice. "A bomb!"

Honourborns screamed. People raced for the exits, stampeding over those not quick enough to stand. Nicholas ran along with the crowd, keeping himself in the middle. Elbows jostled into his side. He winced, but part of him enjoyed the frantic rush. This must be how soldiers felt, energised by the valour of a charge!

"Come on, Callers!" yelled a familiar voice. "Get up, the seven of you!"

Nicholas stumbled, but he kept his balance. That was K, down in the room below. She'd told him she would call out a number. Seven meant the plan was unchanged. Following her orders, he would mark four men and three women, up here in the ballroom.

He pulled another one of K's supplies from his pocket. She'd called it a chemtab, and it was made from two thin sheets of plastic, with an inked outline pressed between them. As Nicholas lurched forward along with the rest of the crowd, he peeled the sticky plastic apart, waiting for the right moment, then grabbed the woman's arm in front of him.

He slapped the plastic onto the back of her left hand. She drew herself away, stumbling. With his enhanced vision, he saw the tattooed marking remain on her skin. It looked quite similar to Zorith's emblem. Nicholas slowed, allowing the crowd to fill the gap between him and the woman. An unnecessary move, anyway, since it was too dark for them to see. Armed with K's serum, only Nicholas possessed his regular sight.

One down and six remaining. K had provided rough descriptions for what his targets should look like, although she'd allowed flexibility for Nicholas to select them himself. Using her information, Nicholas had chosen likely candidates earlier in the night.

He moved through the terrified crowd. Stealthy, quick, subtle. He'd prove that she had made the right decision by choosing him as the High Captain's spy. With a smile on his handsome face, Nicholas went to work.

Chapter 30: From Her Slumber

"Is she awake?"

Pain throbbed through Kef's skull. She groaned. Every inch of her ached and her swollen tongue felt too big for her mouth. Darkness surrounded her. Dead? No, too painful for that. Gritting her teeth, she opened her eyes. The darkness grew a little lighter, but still remained. Something pressed against her face. A blindfold? She tried reaching up to remove it, but cold metal tugged against her wrists, keeping her arms locked behind her back. Handcuffs.

"She's awake. Take it off."

Fingernails scraped against her forehead. They ripped the blindfold off, flooding light into her eyes. Kef squinted.

After a few moments, her eyes adjusted to the brightness. She sat at the prow of a boat with her wrists handcuffed behind her. Dozens of soldiers stood before her, with Exoran at the lead. The sky was a pale grey, despite the sun burning its way up from the horizon. Early Fallsday morning. She must've been unconscious for hours.

Kef tried to stand, to launch herself at Exoran, but something jarred against her handcuffs, keeping her pinned to the deck. She growled.

"No more tricks," said Exoran. "Guards, shoot her if she

tries to escape."

Kef slumped back against the ground, glaring up at her captors. Underneath her, the boat swayed as it glided across the water.

"Where are you taking me?" she asked.

Her words were mumbled and drool flew from her mouth as she spoke. Wincing, she worked her jaw, trying to see if anything was broken. Certainly felt that way. Hopefully, it was just bruised.

"To your execution," said Exoran. "And to mark a new era for Zorith."

The rising sun shone across his handsome face as he gazed at Kef. She twisted around to see the Lightning Tower, gleaming in the early morning light. Their boat was circling around Zorith, probably heading towards the Half-Flood Plaza, where most executions were held.

"Executions and I don't pair so well." Said Kef. "Ask Warden Henderson."

"The Warden has caused almost as much chaos as you. After that incident at the Alchemical Factory, I returned him to Blackrake." Exoran crouched so that his eyes were on Kef's level. "Still, I wouldn't be so glib if I were you, thief."

"And if I were you, I wouldn't gloat." Kef rolled her head from side to side, feeling her neck creak. "So, are you getting to it?"

"Getting to what?"

"I'm still alive. There's something you want from me."

Exoran sniffed. "Within the hour, you will be dead by an executioner's hand. Nothing you can say or do will change that."

Kef smirked. "But?"

"You do have the chance to decide how painful your ending will be. My executioners can make your death last a second or a day."

Kef yawned. "Sounds like fun."

"You jest because you are afraid."

"I jest because otherwise you're the only joke on this boat."

"As I say, you decide what agony you will endure today. Tell me who you're working for and how you got into the Tower, and I'll make your death quick."

Kef tried to shrug, but the handcuffs stopped her. "Why didn't you say that earlier? I was going to tell you everything, anyway. Such a successful plan deserves for the world to know."

"Your plan failed. The Lightning Callers are still in the Tower, and you are about to die."

Kef glanced at the guards. None of them seemed shocked by Exoran talking about the Callers.

"Ah, I see why we're on this boat." Kef nodded to the soldiers. "You actually trust all of them, don't you? Smart. Now I can't embarrass you by sharing the truth about the Tower. Very clever. You should run a city, sometime. Oh wait, you do! And you only had to kill a few hundred people to get there."

Exoran bowed his head. "You don't understand. The other city-ships were planning to attack us, but now they'll reconsider. Zorith is strong again."

"Mmm, almost, except for that last bit."

Exoran glanced at the timepiece on his wrist. "We arrive at the Plaza in ten minutes."

"Oh, right, me telling you the plan, stopping the painful death, got it, got it. So, my employer was …" Kef winced. "Tried to point at myself there, but my hands are tied. No chance you could free them?"

"No chance." Exoran's eyes were cold as steel. "You expect me to believe that you did it all yourself?"

"I had some help, but yeah. All me."

"Is your employer Daen?"

Kef had never heard that name before. "Who?"

Exoran's lips pressed together. "I'm asking the questions. And I'm yet to receive a decent answer. How did you get into the Lightning Tower?"

Kef frowned. "Well … I asked very politely if it would open up, and then I slipped inside. The same approach served me well with your mother."

Exoran's slap made light explode behind her eyes, and as her head crashed against the ground, she blacked out. Kef's eyes shot open an instant later, gasping. A soldier yanked her up by her hair, ramming her back to a sitting position.

"At this stage, your death will last until noon," Exoran said. "Better answers, please."

"Yeah, you're right. See if I can reach midnight."

Kef glanced up at the sky. Thin grey streaks of clouds rolled over Zorith, casting shadows over the city-ship. Looked like that execution would be happening in the rain.

"Okay, I'll give you the real answer, but only because you're so nice," she said. "I detonated a bomb around the Tower's base to distract the gillers, then I swam underneath and crawled through the water intake pipes. From there, it was fairly straightforward to sneak up through the rest of the ship to find the Lightning Callers. Apart from a few distractions along the way. Annoying guards, a ton of stairs, oh, and – of course – your daughter."

Exoran flinched. "What?"

"Didn't she tell you? Your darling girl was playing hide and seek in a stairwell. Pathetic hider, between you and me. You really ought to –"

Exoran pulled his gun from his holster, pointing it at her. The weapon trembled in his hand.

"What did you do to her?"

Kef laughed. "Nothing. My quarrel is with you."

"Yes … of course." Exoran put the gun away, his chest heaving. "I would have been told if she was hurt … yes, she's fine …"

"I wouldn't say that. Seemed like an arrogant little bastard to me."

Exoran's nostrils flared. His hand reached again to his gun, but he stopped himself from drawing it. Instead, he smoothed the wrinkles in his jacket.

"Once you got the Callers, how were you planning to escape?" he asked, only the barest hint of anger in his voice.

"Can't answer that question."

"Then you can add another three hours to your death."

"Let me clarify. I can't answer that because your question's wrong."

"What?"

"See, when it's a hypothetical, you say, *planning*. But it's not. It's history. You should've asked: how *did* they escape?"

"I don't know what ludicrous rubbish you're saying, but if I were you, I wouldn't be wasting my time –"

"There's been no lightning strikes since the explosion, have there?"

Exoran's jaw twitched. Behind him, some of the guards exchanged frowns.

"The Callers are … resisting." He pointed up at the darkening skies. "But that won't last long."

Kef grinned. "I think it'll last a while. Forever, actually. Because there's no Lightning Callers left in the Tower."

Exoran stared at her for a long moment. Behind him, the guards whispered to each other and a few of them fidgeted with their uniforms.

Then Exoran laughed. "You think that you're so clever, but you're a fool."

Her smile wavered. "What?"

"I realised what you were attempting, and I stopped it."

"Yeah, right –"

"Shut up, thief." His nostrils flared. "I've been dealing with arrogant fools like you all week. I'm sick of it. You're all so smug, so entitled, so convinced that you're some gift to the world, but you aren't as clever as you think. I know exactly what you tried in the Tower. After you broke into the Surge room, you blew a hole in the ceiling. The lights cut out. Before the guards could break inside, the Callers swapped with honourborns from the ballroom above. You changed their clothes, their shoes, even gave them the exact names of the people they switched with. Credit to you, I don't know how you did it. But you made one mistake."

Exoran raised his arm, pointing to the back of his left hand. "You forgot their tattoos."

Kef blinked.

"What?" she croaked.

A savage smile spread across Exoran's face. "We mark our Callers, thief. The emblem of Zorith is tattooed on their hands. After you switched them, the Callers did a convincing act of pretending to be honourborns. Their disguises still remain – alchemical, I presume – and some even duped the more foolish bystanders into vouching for them, although the rest of the party were too sensible to get involved. But no matter how much they protested, they couldn't hide their markings. We swapped them back. Right before we dragged you out of the room. It was a little embarrassing, but executing you will show I'm still fit to rule."

Kef stared at the deck. "Oh."

"You failed," said Exoran. "Not so smug now, are you?"

The guards chuckled. Thunder rumbled in the distance and a fine mist of rain fell against Kef's cheeks. She looked up at Exoran. He'd controlled Kef's entire life. Even when she had escaped him, he'd still had power over her – power over her dreams and her nightmares, power too strong for her to overcome.

"See?" Exoran gestured up at the darkening clouds. "The storm returns to serve our city. Zorith prevails!"

The guards cheered. Rain grew heavier, splattering against the deck. Exoran's chest heaved with triumph. Bags hung under his red-rimmed eyes, and judging by his stinking coffee breath, he hadn't slept much in these last few days, but this victory seemed to fill him with energy.

Damn it. She just couldn't hold it in anymore.

Kef laughed so hard she doubled over, tears dribbling down her nose, snorting and gasping for air. By the time she got it under control, all the guards were staring at her. Some had stepped back. Others were holding rifles, frowns creased across their faces.

Exoran's brow furrowed. "Are you mad?"

"I'll tell you what I am, soon. But first – oh, Exoran. This storm isn't for you."

Another boom of thunder shook the skies. Their boat had

turned around enough to place half the city-ship between them and the Lightning Tower. Lightning flashed, missing the Tower's spire.

"My plan worked perfectly." Kef leaned forward, straining at her handcuffs. "We didn't swap the Callers and the honourborns."

"What? But – the tattoos –"

"I removed them from the Callers, and my agent put them on the honourborns. You swapped them for me. Those Callers in the Tower – they're honourborns. And the real Callers? Released from the Tower along with the rest of your party, and already sailing away from this stupid city-ship. You'll never find them again."

"No." Exoran gaped. "But that's impossible. Look, the lightning's coming back –"

More lightning flashed nearby, missing the Tower. Thunder quaked the air. Soldiers flinched and a few superstitious ones made warding signs with their hands.

"You couldn't have told them this!" Exoran said, shouting over the pouring rain. "My guards were outside. They heard everything you said!"

"But not everything I *told* them. One of the Callers is deaf; all of them know sign language. That's how I shared my real plan. When they pretended to betray me, it was so they could get the supplies from my backpack, remove their tattoos, and let guards swap them with the honourborns. There were more notes in my pack for the finer details."

"No! No, that's not possible, no one could know about that, except …" Exoran's voice faded. "Wait …"

Kef bared her teeth. "You still don't recognise me?"

"What? Who are you?"

235

"My name was Katie. You stole me from my parents, branded me with your mark, and trapped me in the Tower. All because I could summon lightning."

Exoran's eyes widened, horror spreading over his face. He shook his head.

"Ten years you drained me," said Kef. "Ten years you tortured me, ten years you kept me locked in that Tower. But then I escaped. I took new names, paid with blood and death. Janice Claw-Arm. Mary the Red. Raider of the Far Reach. Kef Cutmark. But none of those names are true. None of those names are truly mine."

"Guards!" Exoran pointed a shaking finger at her. "Aim – aim your weapons!"

An ear-splitting crack sounded above them. Lightning struck the water beside their boat with a white-hot flash, spraying water over the railing, splashing onto the soldiers, making them slip onto the rain-slicked deck. Exoran's boots flew out beneath him. He collapsed onto his backside. Kef stuck out her tongue to taste the ocean's spray.

Cold. Sweet. Perfect.

"I promised to tell you who I am," said Kef, her voice carrying over the roaring wind. "I'm the storm. And the storm can't be caged."

Kef arched back, gazing up at the sky. Rain hammered onto her cheeks, wind ripped at her hair, and dark clouds rolled overhead, casting the boat into shadow.

Exoran stumbled up, boots sliding in the wet. "Guards –"

Brightness flashed in the sky. A lightning bolt arced down from the clouds to strike Kef. Her body burst aflame, her blood turned to liquid fire, and she laughed, inhaling the sharp smell of ozone, feeling energy crackle across her skin. As Exoran screamed and raised his gun, she looked into his eyes and allowed pain to overwhelm her senses.

With a burst of fury, she made the electricity explode.

Epilogue

E liza glanced to the yacht's starboard side, trying to keep herself distracted. She'd heard the sun set in the west, but after living a life in the windowless Tower, she had no real idea how that worked. Everything was a strange new wonder, from the crests of waves behind their yacht, to the seagulls soaring through the air, to the changing light of the sky.

When their boat had left Zorith, she'd drunk in those wonders like she was dying from thirst. They were still glorious to her; she hoped they'd stay glorious forever. Although now that they'd been anchored to a reef for two hours with no sign of Katie's arrival, darker thoughts were pressing in on Eliza.

The grumpy old woman who called herself an architect – Gabine was her name – glanced at her timepiece. Eliza had never seen one of those before, either.

"Kef promised to arrive by sunset," Gabine said.

Eliza couldn't hear the elderly woman, of course, but she could read her lips, even if she wasn't enunciating as clearly as the other Callers did.

"What did Katie ... Kef, sorry ... say to do if she didn't get here by then?" Samu asked, rubbing his wrinkled face.

Gabine chewed her lip. "She said to leave."

Eliza swallowed. At times like this, she almost wished she couldn't read lips.

Water sprouted from behind the boat. A rough curve of barnacle-encrusted skin slid out from under the waves. Eliza gaped. A whale! A real live whale, right next to their boat! She watched with wide eyes as the creature slid back underwater.

Eliza had read about whales in books, of course. She'd read about everything in books. Of endless waters, graceful boats, and dashing heroes. Despite all that she'd read, none of it seemed real. Especially the bit about heroes. But what Katie had done last night … it had felt so unreal, like something they'd read together in one of their storybooks, back when they were both girls. Yet it *was* real. They were free. This yacht was bigger than the room she'd spent almost her entire life inside. And it was real!

She smiled at the other six Lightning Callers, who were huddled around her on the yacht's main deck. Strange, how they crowded together in one corner, even with all this extra room to spread out. How long would it take to change their habits? It would be particularly difficult for Samu, who'd been in the Tower since it opened three decades ago. Still, Eliza knew they would be fine. As long as they stayed together, and stayed positive, they would make it through anything. She just knew it.

Around them, the ocean was calm and empty, with no boats as far as her poor-sighted eyes could see. The sun reddened as it sunk towards the horizon. How long until it vanished? All this was so strange to Eliza, but the bald man who was steering the boat – Harold – said it would dip below the waters in fifteen minutes. He'd even signed it for her, which had made Eliza smile.

239

Fifteen minutes. Eliza squinted at the horizon, looking in the direction where she thought Zorith was. Or was it the other way?

What she was really worried about was Katie. Or Kef, which was what Harold called her. Truthfully, Eliza didn't care what name the others were using, because Eliza would always think of her as Katie. Was she okay? Yew had meant to hit her – Katie had been clear on that – but what if he'd hit too hard? What if he'd … no, Eliza wouldn't even consider that. Positive thoughts, like Samu always said.

"It's almost set," said Yew. "We should move. They'll be searching for us."

Gabine looked down at her timepiece again. "We've still got ten minutes. And … Kef has something I need."

"Every second we wait increases the risk. Kef is probably delayed. Or dead."

Eliza stood, her body trembling.

Katie freed us, she signed. *You said that was impossible. If she can do that, we can wait for her.*

Yew raised his eyebrows. "Didn't hear you. Your hands were shaking."

Eliza scowled. She strode forward to give Yew a piece of her mind. Samu stood between them, raising his arm. For a second, Eliza wondered if she could dart around the old man to hit Yew, but even her hardest punch probably wouldn't make Yew flinch. Sighing, Eliza turned back to her seat.

And there in the distance was a boat, gliding towards them.

Eliza's eyes widened. She pointed. The others followed her gesture and then they all sprinted towards the railing, waving at the boat. Eliza ran after them. She squeezed between Thamar and Flora and her heart soared. It was Katie! Bloodied

240

and drenched with water, her little boat puttering a cloud of smoke into the air. Eliza clapped her hands, cheering. Beside her, the others joined in. Their applause made her elated, even if she couldn't hear their clapping, because it was the greeting Katie deserved.

She docked beside their yacht. A second, smaller boat was hitched behind her dinghy, bobbing in the water. Wincing, Katie clambered over the railing, slinging a bag onto the deck, a tired smile on her weathered face. Eliza still couldn't believe how tanned she was. Eliza's skin was milk-white. Katie's had once been the same.

Katie strode over to Harold and Gabine, handing Harold the bag.

"Everything's in here," she said. "New identities for you, Gabine, and for the Callers. Along with enough luras to start your new lives. And, Harold –"

She handed him keys. "This is for the second boat, so you can go back to Zorith. Thank you."

Harold accepted the keys from Katie, patting her on the shoulder. "Don't thank us. This was your work."

Katie shook her head. "It was all of our work."

Harold farewelled Gabine, then said goodbye to the Lightning Callers. A lump formed in Eliza's throat.

Thank you, she signed.

He smiled back at her. The lump grew larger. Eliza had only known him for a day, but she still felt sad as Harold stepped into Katie's second boat and started the engine. He glided away. Eliza waved until he disappeared behind the waves.

A hand tapped her shoulder. Eliza turned. When she saw Katie's face, she beamed. Katie stepped forward, embracing her, and Eliza buried her nose in Katie's hair. She smelled of oil and salt. Eliza didn't care what she smelled like, because after all this time, they'd finally been reunited.

They slipped apart, gently.

Where are we going? Eliza signed.

"Someplace safe." Katie gestured at Gabine. "She has a map, and new identities for all of you. There's plans in the folder, too, for if you want to stay together or go your own ways. You'll be safe. Even … even I won't be able to find you."

Eliza gaped. *You're not coming with us?*

Katie looked down. "I can't."

Yes you can. Eliza's heartbeat quickened. *If you can free us from the Tower, you can do anything*!

She tilted Katie's head back up. Tears shone in the girl's eyes. No, she wasn't a girl anymore. She was a woman, tall and strong, years removed from the child who'd played with Eliza in the Tower – the girl who'd read her stories when she was young and acted as the characters when Eliza grew old enough to read by herself.

"I thought freeing you would make me …" Katie's voice trailed away. "Look, what matters is that you're free."

Eliza gulped. An emptiness gnawed at her, making her feel like the deck was dissolving under her feet. Her mind raced. Surely there was something she could declare to make Katie realise she could stay. In the stories they'd read together, nothing was ever impossible to solve, and even the worse horrors could be fixed with the right words. But this wasn't one of her storybooks. If those words existed, Eliza couldn't find them.

Heat flushed Eliza's cheeks as Katie turned away from her to farewell the rest of the crew. They looked sad, but not shocked.

Katie climbed into her little boat and Eliza stumbled to the railing, reaching out to her. Katie glanced at her hand, then looked down at her own. Eliza shut her eyes, not wanting her tears to be the last thing Katie saw. Katie didn't deserve that.

A course hand brushed against her fingers. Eliza opened her eyes to see Katie grasping her hands, staring into Eliza's eyes. Eliza squeezed back. In that squeeze, she tried to thank Katie for the joy she'd created, the laughs they'd shared, their tiny escapes into imaginary worlds, and – above everything – she tried to thank Katie for the best escape of all.

Tears dripped down Katie's cheeks. She nodded. Eliza knew she understood. Katie released her, letting her fingers slip away, but leaving something in her hand. As Katie untied her boat, Eliza looked down, unfolding her fingers.

It was a bracelet made from frayed rope.

Eliza gasped, putting her fingers to her mouth. She'd made this for Katie so long ago that she had almost forgotten it existed, but seeing it brought back all the memories they'd forged together. Joy burst through her heart. Eliza fixed the bracelet around her wrist and warmth spread through her.

Katie nodded. A small, contented smile formed on her lips. Her boat drifted apart from Eliza, and then she glided away, bobbing across the waters of the Twisted Seas, sailing towards the sunset.

Keep exploring the Twisted Seas ...

Kef's adventures continue in *Hunt the Fallen Sky (Twisted Seas #2)*, where she must reunite the fractured Sea Scars crew to salvage a relic fallen from the Debris Belt that orbits Entoris.

Currently scheduled to release mid-2021.

To be notified when *Hunt the Fallen Sky* releases, please sign up to Jed Herne's newsletter at:

www.JedHerne.com/TwistedSeasNews

As a thank you for signing up, you'll also receive free stories from Jed Herne, along with artwork and special behind-the-scenes insights into the world of the Twisted Seas.

Jed Herne is a fantasy author from Perth, Western Australia. His books include *Fires of the Dead*, *Across the Broken Stars*, and *The Thunder Heist*.

He also hosts The Novel Analyst Podcast; The Half-Baked Stories Improvised Storytelling Podcast; The Jed Herne Audio Experience; and the Wizards, Warriors, & Words fantasy writing advice podcast. Yup, he likes talking.

Visit his website for a free story, and to join his email newsletter for regular updates and behind-the-scene exclusives:

www.JedHerne.com/FreeStory

Acknowledgments

First off, a huge thank you to my family for all your wonderful support and love. A particularly big thanks to my Dad, Keith, for his wonderful proofreading.

To David, for all the walks, encouragement, and wisdom. You've played a huge role in helping me pursue my writing dreams.

To Rob J. Hayes, Michael R. Fletcher, and Dyrk Ashton – our *Wizards, Warriors, and Words* podcast has been a highlight of 2020, and you've all taught me a lot about the craft. More importantly, thank you for further stoking my excitement for writing. Thank you to all the other authors I've interacted with or been inspired by – through podcast interviews, twitter chats, or just by becoming utterly enraptured in your stories. Special mention to fellow Aussie author Gabriel Bergmoser for helping me with some big career-affecting decisions.

On the production side, thanks to Rebekah for being an amazing editor, who once again went above and beyond to craft this story into something great. Likewise, thanks to Tina for your exceptional work with the logo, and to Ramon for your incredible cover art.

And lastly, to you, the reader! This is the first of many adventures I want to write about Kef and the Twisted Seas. I hope you've enjoyed the ride, and I hope we can keep following her journey together.

Please Leave a Review

If you enjoyed *The Thunder Heist*, I would massively appreciate if you could please leave an honest review on Amazon or Goodreads. Reviews encourage new readers to try my books, so it's a great way to help more people discover Kef Cutmark and the Twisted Seas. Thanks!

ACROSS
THE
BROKEN
STARS

JED HERNE

Across the Broken Stars
by Jed Herne

Leon has a secret. He was once an angel – a winged warrior sworn to protect Paya, a realm where people live on discs that float in space.

He failed.

Now, Leon's a broken man, trying to forget the past. He thinks he's the last angel. But then a young fugitive stumbles onto Leon's doorstep. She's an angel, too. And she has a riddle leading to a place where angels still live. Or so the stories claim ...

Desperate for redemption, Leon begins a perilous quest through myth and folklore. But will Leon and the fugitive find their legendary destination? Or will Leon lose his last chance for salvation?

Get your copy at:

www.JedHerne.com/AcrossTheBrokenStars

"The details that went into the creation of this world were fantastic." – Darian Seese.

"[Leon's] actions and emotions are so achingly normal which is something rarely seen in fantasy novels." – Jaimee Camilleri.

"If you are looking for an epic fantasy that has a unique setting, this is it." – Kate Valent, Reedsy Discovery Starred Review.

FIRES OF THE DEAD

JED HERNE

Fires of the Dead
by Jed Herne

A thieving sorcerer makes one last grasp for glory.

Wisp is old. Too old for a thief, too old for a sorcerer, and too old to heal all the scars he's torn in the world. He needs to retire, and he needs it soon.

Rumours have spread that a sorcerer's skull is hidden in a desolate, haunted forest. And people will pay big money if that rumour turns into truth.

Wisp leads a misfit thieving crew into the forest, hoping to win the riches he so badly deserves. But when rivals descend upon the forest and nightmares come to life, he'll need all his old tricks to survive – and some new ones, too.

Wisp might be long in the tooth, but he can still bite. Or at least that's what he hopes …

Get your copy at:

www.JedHerne.com/FiresOfTheDead

"Fires of the Dead proves that you don't need to write reams of narrative to fit all the components of a classic fantasy novel into one tale." – Reviews Feed

"The perfect read for someone looking to be quickly immersed in a magic system unlike anything else." - Synopses by Sarge

"I honestly did not put this one down til I finished." - From Cover to Cover

Printed in Great Britain
by Amazon